THRONE OF THORNS

A TRANSYLVANIAN HISTORICAL FANTASY

THE CURSE OF THE DRACULA BROTHERS
BOOK ONE

RR JONES

APOLODOR PUBLISHING

CHAPTER I
THE PROPHECY

Nuremberg, Germany, January 1431

A harsh blizzard smelling like smoke and snow slams the shutters of the timbered houses and bends the moaning trees into submission. Nuremberg's cobblestoned streets are empty, but for the lone rider bundled up in his fur-trimmed cloak.

It's so late it's early, Vlad thinks, tightening his knees around his horse to urge him on. He watches the moon go down with a smile. His belly's full of wine, his heart bursts with hope, and his head brims with plans for the future.

The winter night is mostly spent by the time he heads home after his meeting with King Emperor Sigismund's butler, the keeper of his most hidden secrets. It took at least four cups of the smoothest Cotnari wine from Moldova to squeeze out of the man that Sigismund, the Holy Roman Emperor and the King of Hungary, Germany, Bohemia, and who knows how many other countries, spoke about naming Vlad the voivode of Wallachia.

That's wonderful news, even if it's only to put God's fear into Dan, the second of his name, Wallachia's current voivode, who got rather cozy with Sultan Murad the second. If only it were true!

God knows it took Sigismund long enough! But if he does it, all Vlad has to do is chase Dan out of Wallachia and grab the throne. That shouldn't be hard once Vlad manages to gather an army. After all, he's no longer a spring chicken. He's almost forty and fought in battle after battle alongside Sigismund; John, the emperor of Constantinople; the Genoese; and even his sanctity, the pope. Grabbing Wallachia's throne from under Dan's ass should be as easy as stealing coins from a blind beggar. Easier still since he wouldn't feel bad about it.

Vlad is so deep in thought he doesn't notice the commotion in the dark alley until he falls upon it. It's a woman with her back to a wall, facing two men coming at her from both sides. She's got nowhere to go, so she melts into the wall, watching them close in.

"C'mon, woman, that purse can't be worth your life," the taller man says in German, pulling a knife from the scabbard tucked inside his belt. "Just drop it, and we'll be on our way."

"Yes. We won't even touch you, though God knows you deserve it after all the trouble you gave us. And for what? For a purse you made out of them suckers in one night. You can do it again tomorrow and the day after that. But my friend here and I, we need the money now," the short man growls.

The tall man shakes his head. "I dunno. You don't get this kind of crowd every day. Still, being poor beats being dead."

He stretches his hand to grab the woman, who hasn't yet moved. She must be frozen by fear, Vlad thinks. He urges his horse toward them, when, faster than a snake uncoiling, the woman stabs the man's arm and pulls back before he gets to scream.

Frozen into place, the stabbed man stares at his bleeding arm. His partner pulls out his knife and steps forward.

"That's enough. Step back, or I'll cut you both," Vlad shouts, pulling his heavy sword out of its scabbard.

The men glare at him for a moment, then turn to run down the dark alley and fade into the shadows. The woman's eyes dart left and right for an escape, but there's none. Vlad and his horse block one side of the alley; the men ran to the other.

"Don't worry, I won't hurt you," Vlad says.

The woman's eyes take him in and she smiles.

"Let me take you home. It's too late for a woman to walk the streets alone," Vlad says.

The woman laughs, and her laugh is clear and joyful like a Christmas sleigh bell.

"It's not too late; it's too early," she answers in Romanian, and Vlad's jaw falls.

He takes in her long flowing skirts, the black hair braided with coins cascading down her back, and the three strings of gold around her neck. She's willowy and dark instead of pink, blonde, and sturdy like most Nuremberg women. She reminds him of the gypsy fortune tellers from his childhood. All but her eyes, which measure him instead of hiding.

"You must be from Wallachia? I'm..."

"Close. I'm Smaranda, from Transylvania. And I know who you are. You're Vlad, Mircea the Elder's bastard, and Emperor Sigismund's right-hand man."

Vlad's heart skips a beat.

"You know me? How come?"

The woman shrugs.

"That's my job. I notice things, and I know people. I earn my living by telling people their fortunes. Amongst other things."

Vlad sighs with relief. He's seen plenty of fortune tellers. They're all nomads who read your future in your palm, the cards, or the fire. They learn something about you, then pile up a load of junk about hidden enemies, looming dangers, and the incredible fortune that awaits you. They promise you'll get rich and famous, then take off with your purse.

Oh well. We all have to live. And the woman was incredibly brave in confronting those armed thieves. Come to think of it, she didn't even seem scared. Good for her.

"I see. Those two attacked you to take the money you earned last night. You were courageous, but they were right. It's not worth dying for one night's earnings, no matter how good. Either way, let me take you home. Then I'll go on my way."

"You're a good man, Vlad. Thank you for your help."

"Of course. Let's go."

Smaranda shakes her head and the coins in her hair ring like bells.

"I'm good. You go home to your wife and your son. They're worried about you, and Doamna Cneajna is not well."

Vlad's breath catches in his throat. How does this woman know his wife's name? But then he remembers all the fuss Sigismund made over them when they arrived last month. To spite Dan, for sure. Still, everyone in Nuremberg must know him by now and know he's a got family. Not like he's kept them secret.

"Thank you, but if you're looking to tell me my fortune, know that I don't have any money."

Smaranda laughs again.

"I know you don't. I don't want your money, but I'll tell you your fortune all the same just because you tried to help me. I didn't need it, but I'm grateful.

The woman touches his knee and closes her eyes. All of a sudden, the night goes quiet. A deep cold seeps into Vlad's bones, and he shivers. He pulls his cloak tighter, as the scent of freshly cut hay warmed by the sun, the smell of his childhood summers, comes out of nowhere and warms him inside.

Her eyes still closed, the woman speaks like she's in a dream.

"Someday, you'll get what you've been yearning for. Not yet, but someday you will.

"But for now, beware. Your worst enemy is on his way. He's younger, stronger, and richer than you, and he'll stop at nothing to destroy you. But your wisdom and your patience will win. For now.

"Before the moon fills again, King Sigismund will name you prince of Wallachia. But that alone won't give you the throne. You'll have to suffer and fight for it. Long, hard, and dirty.

"Before the year's end, your wife will give you another son. A son that will carry your name for generations to come and make people shiver. A son whose name will mean blood, fear, and darkness for a thousand years.

"But that's far away. For many years, you'll be away from your home, fighting a fight that isn't yours and waiting to sit on your father's throne. But, through betrayal, another one of your blood will steal it from you.

"And still, someday you'll get your heart's desire. Years from now, the mother of your sons will help you sit on Wallachia's throne of thorns. And after you, so will your sons. All five of them. And they will all, to the last one, lie, betray, and kill for it. Just like you.

"Still, a thousand years from now, men who have never heard of Wallachia, King Sigismund, or even Sultan Murad will shiver when they hear your name. Vlad Dracul, your name will live forever."

The woman opens her eyes that glow in the dark like two moons. Vlad shivers and tries to say something, but his throat is so dry he can't speak.

The thunder roars as the woman lifts her arms and disappears.

CHAPTER 2
A LITTLE FAMILY

The hoarse roosters are done calling the morning, and a hundred plumes of smoke rise from skinny chimneys by the time Vlad finally gets home. As the king's guest and a family man, he lives in one of the timbered houses lining the palace's courtyard, which is good. Here, they're close enough to feel like they belong but separate enough to be their own little family.

He should have been back hours ago, but that strange woman's words rattled him to the core. He needed time to think, so he cantered through the empty streets of Nuremberg all the way to the Tiergarten Gate, then left the fortress for the frozen fields. He urged his horse and galloped with the wind in his face until his hands froze on the reins, and Viscol, his old gray stallion, turned white with spume. Only then, tired and weary, did he turnaround and trot back, avoiding the street merchants selling roasted chestnuts and mulled wine who gave him weary looks. No wonder. He had to look frightful.

He drops Viscol off at the king's stables and walks home, but he still doesn't know what to think. He starts wondering if that woman

Smaranda was real or just a creation of his mind born of too much wine and endless hope. How else could she vanish the way she did?

Unless she's a witch...

People whisper that there are plenty of witches in Nuremberg, but they stay hidden. And that's no wonder. These days, the holy men of the church have no higher mission than burning witches at the stake. Unless they drown them, of course. They say that's the only sure way to tell if they're witches. If they drown, it means they were innocent. It they don't, they've got to be witches, so they burn them at the stake. But now that it's winter and the lakes are frozen, the fire's the way to go.

Vlad is still pondering Smaranda's prophecy as he gets home. He lowers his head to clear the wooden door and steps in. It's almost midmorning, but the kitchen is empty, and the fireplace cold. A dagger of fear stabs his heart, and he wonders if Dan, Alexandru, or some other enemy got to those he holds dear. But no.

"Father? You're back!"

His curly black hair messed up from sleep, little Mircea rushes in from the sleeping room, his tiny feet pattering on the worn wooden floor like hail. He hugs his father's knees, and Vlad picks him up.

"How's my boy? Have you been good?"

Mircea nods, his dark eyes serious.

"Yes. Mama told me to stay in bed, and I did. She's sick."

Vlad remembers the witch. "Doamna Cneajna is not well," she had said. He shivers and walks into the bedroom that's barely big enough for the four-poster bed they all share.

"Doamna?"

In the small windows' meager light, Doamna Cneajna's drawn face is almost as white as the linen bedsheets. Still, she opens her tired, hazel eyes and smiles. She hasn't been well for weeks, ever since she got heavy with child, but she never complains.

"You're back! Good. I've been worried."

"It was a long night."

"How did it go?" Cneajna asks.

"As well as one could expect. The man said Sigismund thinks about naming me voivode of Wallachia. That would be timely since the last messenger we got from Târgoviște said that the boyars are getting tired of Dan. A few of them have started to stir and talk about getting a new voivode. Most of them look at my half-brother Alexandru Aldea, but with a bit of luck and lots of cunning..."

"But isn't King Sigismund's blessing enough? What do you need the boyars for?"

Vlad sighs and shakes his head. Doamna Cneajna may be the daughter of Alexandru cel Bun, Moldova's voivode, and not hard to look at. Still, as for understanding the intricacies of politics, she might as well have been born in a stable.

But it's not her fault. She's barely twenty, fifteen years younger than him, and she's a woman. Thank God she can read and write. That's all a noble girl ever learns — other than sewing, cooking, and keeping her husband's household. But then, what else does she need? Politics is for bright minds, not for women.

Still, she's the mother of his son, with another one coming if the witch had it right. She'll need to bring them up and teach them until they're old enough to learn from the men, so he'd better train her now.

"Being named Wallachia's voivode is not the same as ruling the country. To get the throne, I need the boyars' blessing. Or an army. I need men, horses, and weapons; for that, I need money. And King Sigismund, God bless him, is lavish with his compliments but God-awful stingy with his purse. For now, I have not one sword to my name other than mine and old Gheorghe's, who's been my right-hand man forever. As for you, my fair lady, besides your royal blood relations and charming good looks, you didn't bring much of a dowry."

Cneajna blushes and looks down. Vlad feels bad.

It's not her fault, of course. When he asked for her hand in marriage, he knew darn well that Moldova's voivode, Alexandru cel Bun, had fathered more children than any man should, voivode or not, so his daughters would bring more goodwill than gold. But after years and years of looking for an advantageous match in every noble house of Europe from Constantinople to Prague, Doamna Cneajna was the best he could find to further his ambitions.

"Still, why isn't going back with the king's blessing enough?" she asks again.

Vlad sighs.

"I wish it were. But my uncle Dan, the second of his name, just took Wallachia's throne for the fifth time. He has no plans to step aside for me, Alexandru Aldea, or any other of the men of royal bone who covet the throne of Wallachia. As for the boyars...."

Doamna Cneajna's eyes widen.

"Dan took the throne for the fifth time? The same voivode? How can that be? My father has been sitting on Moldova's throne for thirty years, and he's still...."

Vlad shrugs.

"Not everyone is as lucky as your father. Or mine, who reigned Wallachia for thirty-two years before God called him to Him. That was then, and this is now. These days, Sultan Murad and King Sigismund play the game of thrones like it's chess. Wallachian princes are nothing but pawns in the clash of the great empires. And once your father loses his grip on the throne, I bet that Moldova will follow suit. Murad and Sigismund change voivodes more often than they change their shirts. As for Transylvania, Hungary swallowed it and spat out its bones long ago."

"So, what will you do?"

Vlad sighs.

"Whatever it takes, my dear. I'll do whatever is needed to take the throne of Wallachia."

He remembers Smaranda's words:

"And still, someday you'll get your heart's desire. Years from now, the mother of your sons will help you sit on Wallachia's throne of thorns. So will your sons, all five of them. And they will, to the last one, lie, betray, and kill for it. Just like you."

CHAPTER 3
THE RIVAL

T he Nuremberg Castle's double cathedral is nothing like the Wallachian churches. Still, the Catholic Sunday mass is just as drawn out and boring as the Orthodox services Vlad used to attend at home. The Catholics have white walls and painted statues instead of smoky icons. Their priests are clean-shaven and dressed in white instead of the black-robed Orthodox monks with their wild unkempt beards. But the rest is just the same. The smell of incense, the thin sound of coins falling into the donation box, and the enraptured expression of the faithful looking up at the priest like he's sent by God are no different.

Vlad shifts his weight from one foot to the other, hoping it's over soon. Lucky Doamna Cneajna! Thanks to her morning sickness, she didn't have to come. Vlad would have gladly slept in, or gone for a canter on Viscol, but he had to come here to please Sigismund and talk him into giving him Wallachia. And God knows that his Father's throne is worth a few tedious hours in church.

So he waits patiently for the service to be over before walking up to Sigismund to remind him. But the king-emperor is too shrewd to promise anything.

"Sure, Vlad, I know you're my faithful vassal, and I can always rely on you. I'm lucky to have your allegiance; I'll think about Wallachia, and I promise you'll be the first to know. But for now, the boyars support Dan. And I can't go against the will of the country. Give me some time, will you?"

Vlad remembers the twenty-odd years he has given Sigismund. He was still a young boy when his father sent him to Sigismund's court as a hostage and token of fealty. Ever since, he's been by the king's side to watch his back, run his errands, and wait.

Still, Sigismund needs more time.

Vlad swallows the first words that come to his mind and smiles.

"Of course, your majesty. I'm at your service, as always. I'll be glad to..."

The sound of a galloping horse covers his voice. It's a lone dusty rider in Wallachian garb who stops his heaving black horse by the gate. The king recognizes him and smiles.

"Look who just arrived! You two know each other, don't you?"

Vlad shakes his head. He doesn't know who that is and doesn't want to. For all he cares, that darn interrupter can ride his horse straight to hell and stay there. But Sigismund has other plans. He smiles that mischievous half-smile he reserves for his nasty little pranks.

"Really? You don't know him? Then it's high time you met. This is your cousin Basarab, the son of Dan the second, the voivode of Wallachia. Come, I'll introduce you."

Sigismund's boots clatter down the cathedral's worn stone stairs. Vlad follows, wishing he were anywhere else. The courtiers' voices fade to silence as they stare with wide-open eyes. They all know Vlad is here to beg for the Wallachian throne that Basarab's father sits on, and they can't wait to see the show.

But Vlad knows better than to make a show of himself. He follows the king with a smile so wide his face hurts, but his heart shrivels with worry. Why is Basarab here now?

The rider jumps off his horse and kneels to kiss Sigismund's hand. His handsome young face and rich velvet clothes look dusty and tired, but his eyes piercing Vlad could melt steel.

He knows who I am and is not surprised to see me here. That's got to be why he came, Vlad thinks, nodding his greeting.

The king embraces Basarab and turns to Vlad.

"What a handsome young man, isn't he? Brave too, and well-learned. He's only seventeen, but he's already looking at a bright future. He hopes to sit on the throne of Wallachia, like his father, someday."

"He's in the right place, then," Vlad says, struggling to keep his voice soft. "No better place than your majesty's court to find one's way to a bright future. I know that only too well."

"Did you hear that, Basarab? Your cousin Vlad is a wise man. It would behoove you to seek his council and heed his advice."

Basarab's face darkens. If looks could kill, I'd be a dead man, Vlad thinks.

"I don't need advice from the traitor who's trying to steal the throne of my father. You think I don't know why you're here? I do, and that's why I came. I'm here to foil your treacherous plans. And, if I have my way, your head will soon fall where your feet are now."

Sigismund laughs.

"Now, now, Basarab. Is that the way to speak to your cousin? He's almost twenty years your senior and has fought more battles than you can count. He may end up teaching you more than you care to learn."

Basarab's pretty mouth narrows under his thin dark mustache, and his hand flies to the hilt of his sword.

Vlad's brain catches fire. He'd love to crush this arrogant little snake into the ground and cut him into tiny pieces, but this is neither the time nor the place. So he digs his nails into his palms and smiles instead.

"Oh, the innocent heat of youth, when you think the whole world's there for the taking, as long as you carry a sword. How touching."

He nods to the king and walks down the steps. He follows the cobblestoned path to the gate with his hand on the hilt of his sword, hoping Basarab dares to attack him. How sweet would that be? He'd finish him in a heartbeat, and nobody could blame him.

But Basarab doesn't. Vlad feels his eyes burning holes in his back as he avoids the dozen beggars gathered by the gate. They're waiting to lighten the dignitaries' purses, but Vlad's purse doesn't need any more lightening.

The blind beggar beyond the gate looks much like the others. He stretches his hand, begging for a coin, while scratching his lice with the other. But his soft voice speaks Romanian, so Vlad stops to dig inside the light purse hanging from his belt.

"God bless you and all of yours, my prince."

The man's eyes dart left and right; then he whispers: "The boyars expect you at the Blind Horse Inn tonight. There's news from home."

Vlad drops another coin into the dirty hand.

"Tell them I'm coming."

CHAPTER 4
THE SECRET MEETING

T hank God it gets dark early in winter, Vlad thinks, wrapping himself tighter in the cloak that makes him as good as invisible in Nuremberg's dark streets. His hand squeezes the cold hilt of his sword as he walks hugging the walls and watching his back. Once in a while, he stops to listen for steps following him, but there's nothing but the screech of weathervanes turning in the wind and hungry rats scurrying through frozen gutters.

Good. Nobody cares about him. The merchants took their wares home for the night to join their families around the dinner table. The armed watchmen walking the fortress's walls are looking for dangers outside, not in here. Whatever their business, the few men still roaming the streets don't want to be recognized any more than Vlad. And it's too late for women. The proper ones are at home, putting their children to bed. As for the others...they work their trade away from prying eyes.

Vlad takes the long way to the Blind Horse Inn, just in case someone followed his trail, but by the time he sees the narrow building's glowing windows, he's sure there's nothing to worry about.

He glances around once more, then pushes the heavy door. The heat, the smell of old beer, and the cacophony of drunken voices hit him like a punch.

The long wooden tables are full of jolly drinkers singing and filling their bellies with sauerbraten and steamy cabbage. The place is packed, but for the small round table in the corner where two silent men cut their worried eyes to the door. Their faces lighten when they see Vlad.

"You're so late I thought you weren't coming," the first one says. He's rail-thin, tall, and dressed in black from head to toe. His dark garb and long, hungry face remind Vlad of the monks at the Dealu monastery who live to pray, and fast half the year. But his father's trusted captain, Spătar Stanciu, eats like a wolf and fights like a bear.

Vlad shrugs.

"I took the long way to shake whatever tail I might have had. But there was nothing."

"Good." Logofat Zorza nods and slams his cup on the table, calling for more beer. His face is flushed and round like he's never heard of fasting, and his eyes shine. He's already had a few. But it takes more than a few beers to trip his father's old secretary, who's known to thoroughly check the goods of every vineyard in Wallachia every year.

Vlad pulls a heavy, high-backed chair and sits facing the door.

"What's up?" he asks.

Logofat Zorza leans closer.

"I just got a messenger from Wallachia. It smells like trouble. Dan's not happy. After bringing his 6,000 archers to help Sigismund win the battle of Golubac, Dan expected something more substantial than thanks. But Sigismund got himself trapped, so he gave all the spoils to the Hungarians that helped him escape. Dan waited and waited for

Sigismund to make things right, but he didn't. That's why some say Dan got cozy with Sultan Murad."

"How cozy is that?"

The fat man shrugs.

"Nobody knows for sure, but there's some noise that Dan promised the Ottomans safe passage through Wallachia to attack Sigismund's Transylvania. Others say no way. They think it's just a rumor the sultan started to muddy the waters and stir discord among Christians."

Vlad takes a sip of his beer. It's watered down and stale. That's why nobody who's somebody ever comes here. They go to better inns, where the beer is strong and the company better. That's why the Blind Horse is the best place for conspirators to meet.

"Isn't that interesting!"

"I thought so. Even more interesting, Dan got so worried that he's thinking about sending over his son Basarab as proof of fealty. The kid is supposed to reassure Sigismund and smooth things out."

Vlad sighs.

"Is that it?"

"Isn't that enough? The boy's just seventeen, but he's good with the horse and the sword. I bet he'll be a thorn in your side, so I thought you should be forewarned."

"I wish I was, but he's here already. I met him today after church. It wasn't pretty. He's as hotheaded as they come, and he'll be nothing but trouble."

"Well then. That's good news. The king will see who's wise and reliable and who isn't. Letting the kid make a fool of himself may strengthen your claim and further our cause," Spătar Stanciu says.

Vlad nods, but his heart is heavy with worry and his head full of suspicion. *Our* cause? It's my cause. You both are with me only because Dan took your lands. If a better prospect comes your way, I bet you'll sell me out at the drop of a hat. Unless you already have. How could that messenger arrive after the kid? That news should have been here long ago. One of you betrayed me. But which?

Vlad looks from one man to the other. They're his father's old dignitaries, and they both fought by Mircea's side, but that doesn't mean they're faithful to Vlad. Why should they be? The dozen contenders fighting for Wallachia's throne all have Mircea's royal blood running through their veins. It's the boyars' prerogative to pick and choose the voivode they want, then ditch him for another.

The buxom innkeeper brings more beer. She leans forward to slam the cups on the table, making sure they notice the soft flesh bursting from her cleavage. She smiles at Vlad.

He drops a coin on the table and waits for her to be gone before asking: "How come the messenger was so late? He should have been here days ago."

The fat man shrugs. "His horse went lame. He had to get another, and that took time."

Vlad nods, but he's wary. He wishes he knew who to trust.

Spătar Stanciu shakes his head. "Maybe. Or maybe he lied, and he slowed down on purpose. Or maybe those who sent him waited until it was too late to do us any good. It's hard to know who to trust these days. You know, Vlad, my mother was just a peasant woman who couldn't read or write. Still, she was wiser than most men and gave me precious advice. Never put all your eggs in one basket, she said, and she was right. For years, you've kept all your eggs in Sigismund's basket, and nothing has come of it. No throne, no army, no recognition. Nothing. It may be time to move on."

"Move on to what?" Logofat Zorza asks.

"Not to what, but to whom. I don't think Sultan Murad will ever trust Dan after seeing him fight alongside Sigismund at Golubac. He may welcome someone else on the throne. Especially someone as experienced and reliable as Vlad. It may be time to change allegiance. With the sultan's help, you could...."

The fat man gasps. "That's treason! If Sigismund hears..."

"He won't. Not from me. Will he hear it from you?"

They fought and fought and got nowhere, but that got Vlad thinking. Should he give up waiting for Sigismund and send word to the sultan?

He's so deep in thought that he's almost home before he hears steps behind him. Somebody's following him, and he knows he didn't bring them from home. Somebody talked more than they should. Hopefully, not to the king; otherwise, Wallachia's as good as gone.

Vlad quickens his pace to grow the distance, then turns right into a dark alley he has no business being in. He holds his breath and melts into the wall with his sword in his hand.

The steps get closer, then slow down and stop. The night is late; the streets empty and quiet. There's no sound other than Vlad's heartbeat and the old timbered houses creaking from the cold.

Holding his breath, Vlad waits until his fingers grow numb on the hilt, but nothing moves. Whoever followed him won't come further.

Maybe it was just someone living here who went home, Vlad tells himself. But he knows better. There was no creaking gate, no slamming door, and no keys screeching in the lock. Nothing but the deep, unsettling silence of someone who knew better than to get too close.

CHAPTER 5

WHERE ARE YOU TAKING ME?

A day passed, then another, then three more. Nothing happened, and Vlad started thinking he'd panicked for nothing when heavy knocks at the door woke him up before dawn.

Vlad grabbed his sword.

"Who's there? And what do you want?"

"A message from King Sigismund. Open the door."

Vlad's eyes darted from the door to the windows. He could squeeze out if need be, but where would he run, half-naked and without his horse? And what would happen to his wife and his son? I may as well take it like a man, he thought, and opened the door.

Half a dozen of Sigismund's men waited with their hands on their swords.

"His majesty wants you now," their captain said.

Vlad's heart skipped a beat. "What for?"

The captain shrugged. "How would I know? He only told me to bring you."

Vlad glanced at the men. Too many to fight. And even if he managed to kill them all, then what?

He pulled on his boots and tightened his wide leather belt then slipped his sword in his scabbard, kissed little Mircea, who smiled in his sleep, and hugged Doamna Cneajna.

"Take care of the boy. If I don't come back, take him to Moldova to your father. Alexandru will keep you both safe. God willing, he and your brothers will teach Mircea how to be a man and a prince and they'll help him take Wallachia someday."

"But…"

"No time for 'but.' I have to go. Can I go in peace, knowing that you'll do everything you can so our son can take the throne he deserves?"

Doamna Cneajna nodded. Vlad kissed her and opened the door. He glanced back to his wife and sleeping son one last time, wondering if he'll ever see them again, then followed the king's men.

"Where are you taking me?"

"To the chapel."

CHAPTER 6

THE ORDER OF THE DRAGON

The flickering lights of two dozen candles throw twisted shadows that chase each other along the stone floor, then crawl up the walls to drown into the darkness of the ceiling. The trembling flames bring life to the holy gilded statues, but the half-dozen knights standing in front of the altar next to Vlad may as well be statues themselves. Their heads lowered, their fingers frozen on the hilts of their swords, they barely breathe as they listen to Sigismund's long recitation.

"You will defend the Holy Roman Empire and protect the German king and his family. You will shield the widows and the orphans with your life. You will spread our Catholic faith and defend it against all heretics and infidels."

A shiver runs through Vlad. He tightens his fists and bites his lip to stop his teeth from chattering, hoping Sigismund gets on with it. They've been here for hours; his feet are frozen, and his stomach growls, reminding him that he had nothing to eat or drink other than the cup of mulled wine the king handed him when the guards brought him to the chapel.

"There. Drink this. It will chase the chill of the morning."

Vlad drained it, wondering if it was his last wine, but the king refilled the cup, then filled his own.

"I bet you're wondering why I brought you here."

Vlad nodded, though he feared he already knew.

"Vlad, I've known you since you were a child, and your father sent you to grow up at my court as a token of fealty. I've seen to your education as a prince and watched you become the undaunted knight you are today. I'm as proud of you as if I were your father. That's why I decided it's time for you to join my most trusted circle. From today until God calls you to His service, you'll belong to my Order of the Dragon. I know nobody more worthy."

Vlad opened his mouth to thank the king but couldn't find the words. He was still struggling to speak when the metal-studded chapel doors opened to let in the other knights. They lined up by his side, and King Sigismund started the ceremony.

That was hours ago, long enough for Vlad's heart to slow down to normal. He started planning his next moves as he listened to the king's tired voice read the manifesto of the Order of the Defeated Dragon he knows so well.

"On ordinary days, as a symbol of belonging to our order, you will wear the green cape of the dragon. But on Fridays and the days of the Passion of the Christ, you'll wear the black cape of mourning to remind you of your duty."

The king's voice breaks. He signals a young page who steps out of the shadows and kneels by his side, presenting the order's insignia on a gold-embroidered pillow.

It feels like a lifetime since Vlad himself helped the king initiate the first batch of noble knights into the secret Order of the Dragon. The knights were all high-born and famous, and young Vlad wondered if a bastard like him could ever hope to join them. But now his faithful service to King Sigismund has finally paid off. God willing, he will earn not only the twisted dragon insignia, but also his father's title of voivode of Wallachia that the usurpers stole from him.

Sigismund meets his eyes and nods. Vlad steps forward and drops to one knee. He lowers his head to allow the king to slip the ribbon with the order's symbol around his neck. It's a golden dragon biting his own tail that's strangling him, while St. George's shield bearing the Holy Cross crushes him into oblivion. That little piece of metal, no bigger than a baby's palm, is about to change Vlad's life. With that dragon around his neck, Vlad is no longer a nobody, just one of Old Mircea's bastards fighting for Wallachia's throne. He's Vlad Dracul, a knight of the Order of the Dragon, the most exclusive secret order in the world whose two dozen illustrious members, all kings, princes, and nobles, swore to help and protect each other like brothers.

Good. I'll need their help, Vlad thinks. Because even if the king names me voivode, a title is nothing but words, whereas my beloved Wallachia is thousands of miles away, and my uncle Dan is sitting pretty in Father's wood-carved throne.

Even worse, the council of boyars wants him there. They'd rather keep Dan, who they know, than try Vlad. To them, Vlad is just a bastard mercenary who's lived his whole life running from Buda to Suceava and from Prague to Constantinople to do King Sigismund's bidding. And like that's not bad enough, he dresses like a foreigner and speaks Hungarian better than his mother-tongue, for God's sake.

And speaking about God. Some even whisper that Vlad abandoned the Wallachian Orthodox God his father and grandfather worshiped and turned to Catholicism to please the king. And the boyars won't have that. No goddamned foreigner shall sit his Catholic ass on Wallachia's throne as long as they have a say in it, and they have a lot to say. Because they hold the lands, the forests, the fishing ponds, and the power. Some even mint their own coins. The boyars are kings of their domains and plan to stay that way.

But Vlad has plans of his own. And with God's help and King Sigismund's blessing, he's going to show them what's what.

CHAPTER 7
THE KIDNAPPING

Vlad Dracul can't wait to share the good news with Doamna Cneajna. She must be worried sick by now, since he's been gone for most of the day. He'll be home in time for dinner, he thinks, rushing to get home before dark. He tears through the narrow streets, avoiding the street merchants, the hurried riders, and the heavy peasants' carts, and blasts through the door.

"Doamna? Mircea?"

Silence.

That's odd. Where can they be? Have they left for Moldova already?

Vlad runs to the bedroom, but that's empty too. And messy. Mircea's rocking horse lays on its side, and the wooden sword he never leaves behind is broken into pieces on the floor.

Vlad's heart freezes. He knows that something terrible happened, but he doesn't know what until he finds the scroll on the bed.

It's paper, sealed with cheap yellow wax and imprinted with one of Sigismund's ducats bearing the Templar's cross instead of a proper seal.

Vlad breaks the seal with shaky hands.

"We took your wife and your son. Come find them tonight after midnight behind the Tiergarten Gate if you want them back. Bring a thousand golden ducats and don't tell a soul if you want them alive."

Vlad's knees melt. He drops on the bed that smells of lavender and honey, like Doamna Cneajna, and puts his face in his hands.

What should I do?

He doesn't have a thousand ducats. He doesn't even have a hundred. He couldn't get that kind of treasure if he sold his horse, his sword, and his soul. And everyone knows it. From Sigismund himself to the stable boys who look after his horse and the women plucking chickens in the kitchen, they all know that Vlad Dracul isn't rich. He's nothing but a beggar at Sigismund's court, even now that he's a Knight of the Dragon. There's no way on earth he could get that money before midnight other than asking the king. And they told him not to tell anyone. So it's not money they want.

What do they want, then?

There's only one explanation: They want him. They want him there, alone. That's why they told him to be there after midnight when nobody's out but those who are up to no good. Outside Tiergarten Gate, after midnight, there'll be nobody to hear him scream.

So there.

They want him? Then they shall have him.

It's not yet midnight when the three watchmen at the Tiergarten Gate open it to let Vlad out. They give him strange glances, but ask no questions. They're used to seeing Vlad coming and going at any time of day or night in his years in King Sigismund's service.

Vlad urges Viscol forward. A few more steps and they're out of the torches' small circle of light. The darkness of the cloudy night embraces them like a cloak.

Good. Vlad jumps off the horse and waits for his eyes to adjust to the darkness. He's way early, so whoever called him here still has to show up. When they come, Vlad would rather have the light at his back.

He waits, one with the darkness, praying that the moon won't come out of the clouds. Please, good God, not yet. He listens to the night, smells the wind, and squints to pierce the darkness, but there's nothing. It feels like hours until he hears hushed voices from somewhere to his left.

"You think he'll come?" someone asks in Romanian.

"He's got to. We have his wife and his son."

"He's late, though."

"Maybe he's looking for the money."

"I hope so. We could surely use a thousand golden ducats. We wouldn't even have to tell the boss about them."

"Divided by three, that makes..."

"Shut up, you stupid. The boy said there was no way he could find the money, so he'll come to bargain. And when he does..."

"Maybe not a thousand, but if he had a hundred, that would still make more than thirty ducats each...."

Vlad sighs. He was right; it's not the money they want. And it's good to know there are three of them. He'd love to know who that boy is who set them to this, but he can't stall anymore. Doamna Cneajna and Mircea must be scared to death, and the moon is about to come out of the clouds. He has to make his move before they see him.

He pinches Viscol's rump. The horse neighs and leaps into the darkness.

The men spring into action. Weapons clang, heavy boots crush the gravel, and an arrow whistles somewhere in the dark.

"Stop. Come back here," a man calls, but his voice turns into a gurgle as Vlad's battle axe splits him into two like a log too thick to catch fire.

"What was that?" the second one asks, then gasps as Vlad's sword severs his windpipe.

Two gone, one left, Vlad thinks. But I'd better be careful. If I kill this one, too, I won't know where to find Cneajna and Mircea.

"If you treasure your life, drop your sword and stay where you are," Vlad says, his voice barely above a whisper.

The man doesn't listen. The gravel crunches under his boots as he breaks into a run. With his sword in his hand, Vlad follows the shadow. The moon's glow is still faint, but to his eyes well-adjusted to the darkness, that's enough. Vlad raises his sword and drops the flat end over the man's shoulder.

A scream of pain breaks the night. The man curses and stumbles, then turns around. His blade catches the moon as it slashes Vlad's arm.

"You dirty bastard," Vlad spits, then slams him with the flat of his sword until he hears bones crack. The blade clangs as it falls to the ground, and the man drops to his feet, begging for his life.

"Pity, please, sire. I didn't mean to hurt you. Don't kill me, please."

"Why on earth not?"

"I...I have a wife and children. They need me."

Vlad's laughter holds no joy.

"How touching. And that's my problem, how?"

"Sorry, sire. Please, be merciful. I'll take you to your wife."

"Now you're talking. I want the name of whoever put you up to this."

"I don't know it, sire; I swear I don't know it. We never even saw his face. He paid us a hundred ducats to get your wife and son and wait for you here, but none of us knew him. Please don't kill me. I'm telling the truth."

"I won't. Stay put now."

Vlad puts his fingers to his mouth and whistles. Somewhere in the darkness, Viscol neighs, then snorts and trots over. Vlad ruffles his fore-lock in welcome, then ties the man's hands and tethers him to the saddle.

"Let's go."

CHAPTER 8
THE STAFF OF OFFICE

The Imperial Castle of Nuremberg isn't big, despite being the seat of the German emperors for hundreds of years. First, because it's a fortress rather than a castle. Whoever built it, planted it on top of the hill to oversee miles and miles of land so the defenders could see the invaders even before they crossed the Pegnitz River. Second, it's almost 400 years old, and they had fewer people in those days. And third, because Nuremberg is just one of the many fortresses the king hops between to keep an eye on his cumbersome subjects. Like tonight.

The throne room is packed with the best of the best, starting with Sigismund himself, dressed to the nines. Instead of his usual fur hat with long flaps that keep his ears warm, Sigismund wears his domed gold crown studded with precious stones. The thing's so big that it leans to one side, shading the king's face, and Vlad wonders what would happen if it fell. Would it dent? Would the rubies, pearls, and sapphires scatter all over the floor, tempting the noble guests to chase them?

He wishes Doamna Cneajna and Mircea were here to see it all, but Cneajna isn't ready. And Vlad wonders if she'll ever be.

It's been weeks, but Vlad hasn't forgotten the overwhelming relief he felt when he found Cneajna and Mircea alive. They were in a carriage nearby, tied and gagged but otherwise seemingly unharmed.

But their souls, like Vlad's, will never be the same. Fortunately, little Mircea is a robust and healthy kid. It took him a while, but he got over his nightmares. He even started going out to play again. But Doamna is a different story. Two days after that terrible ordeal, she started bleeding. She lost the baby she carried, and she's heartbroken.

"Don't worry, you're young and healthy, and you'll have another one before you know it," the midwife said.

Doamna Cneajna burst into tears and wouldn't stop, no matter what.

Vlad Dracul didn't know what to do.

"I'm sorry, my lady, but did you hear the woman say that you'll soon have another?"

Doamna Cneajna sobbed even louder.

"I don't want another. I want this one," she cried, soaking the pillows in tears.

Vlad sighed. He wiped her tears and held her until she fell asleep, then went to see Sigismund.

The king shared his sympathy, but had no help to offer. Vlad needed answers, and the king had none.

"I'm sorry, Vlad, but I had the man questioned every which way. I got nothing. I even promised to set him free if he gave me the name of whoever put them to do it, but he wouldn't. I bet he doesn't know it," Sigismund said.

"He may not know it, but I do," Vlad said, his heart ugly with hatred.

"Who?"

"Basarab. I know it's him. It can't be anyone else."

"Sure it can. I hate to break it to you, my friend, but you've made plenty of enemies in your many years of manly adventures. There are those you beat in battle, those you outwitted, and those whose wives warmed your bed. Then your rivals: your half-brother Alexandru, who'd love to throw you out of the race for Wallachia's crown. And your uncle Dan, who knows you're claiming his throne."

"It's my throne."

Sigismund smiled. "Not yet, my friend. Someday, maybe, but not yet."

"Either way, I know it's Basarab who did it. I know it in my heart."

The king sighed. "Do you have any proof?"

Vlad shook his head. Sigismund shrugged.

"Well then. I can't punish the kid based on suspicion alone. Find me the proof."

Vlad looked and looked but found nothing.

Still, the king had a change of heart. And that's what tonight's celebration is about. After years and years of empty promises, Sigismund finally decided to make Vlad voivode of Wallachia and invited the empire's best of the best to attend. And they couldn't refuse.

That's why mustached Hungarian counts rub shoulders with colorful Bohemian knights. The Burgrave of Nuremberg, Friedrich von Zolern, stands way too close to Klaus von Redwitz, the Grand Master of the Teutonic order. The few boyars who fled Wallachia to escape Dan the second's wrath, easy to recognize by their byzantine garb and thick furs, elbow each other to get closer to the action.

Their breaths mist the air as they watch the king hand Vlad the Staff of Office, declaring him Prince of Wallachia.

"Vlad, son of Mircea, knight of the Order of the Dragon, our great vassal, and brother, we are thrilled to grant you the title of Prince of Wallachia. We trust that when you take your throne, you will protect our brothers of the Catholic faith, especially the Franciscan Minorites, even though Wallachia still celebrates the Orthodox faith."

Vlad swore he would. What else could he do?

"I swear allegiance to the Emperor, my Natural Lord and Sovereign, at whose Court we all gathered to accomplish great things," he said. He hopes he'll figure out how to protect the Catholics and accomplish all those great things, whatever they were. Someday.

But for now, he must find a way to snatch that throne from under Dan's ass. He'd much prefer that Sigismund give him an army than the darn Staff of Office and words of encouragement in exchange for his fealty.

But to each its time. He'll ponder that tomorrow. For now, it's time to celebrate his win and show these stuffy Catholics who Vlad Dracul is.

CHAPTER 9

THE CHALLENGE

B ut the celebration doesn't end in the castle. Tonight, the whole city of Nuremberg is having a huge party. Spark-spitting bonfires crackle and pop, spreading festive lights along the cobblestoned streets. Long bands of colored bunting adorn the wood-framed houses' high windows and hang along the covered bridges across the winding Pegnitz River. Merchants flushed with beer and mulled wine dance with well-fed women in the public squares. Dozens of mimes, jugglers, snake-oil sellers, and stealthy cut-purses ply their trade in the narrow streets. One way or another, they squeeze silver coins with Sigismund's effigy out of the laughing crowds feasting in front of St. Sebald's church at the bottom of Kaisersburg Hill. But that's all for the masses. They don't know or care what this celebration is about. Those who really matter gathered elsewhere.

Late at night, the whole court gathers around the sparkling bonfires built outside Tiergarten Gate for the tourney. It's a special occasion, and the king spared no expense. His carpenters built stands for the king, his nobles, and the court ladies so they can see, hear, and smell everything. They'll miss nothing, from the angry clang of metal against metal to the maddened eyes of frightened horses and the feral smell of their sweat. They can feel the earth tremble under the hooves without risking getting blinded by an errant splinter or trampled by a riderless horse.

It is, indeed, a sight to behold. Vlad last saw something like this almost twenty years ago, in his last tourney in Gournay-Sur-Aronde. He wishes Doamna Cneajna and Mircea were here to watch. But he and the other knights of the empire won't be watching. Heavily armored and armed to the teeth, the knights will compete to show off their courage and equestrian skills, honor their family banners, and charm the tender-hearted maidens.

Mulled wine flavored with cinnamon and sweetened with honey flows like water in the stands to keep the cold at bay. Above his steaming cup, the king's sparkling eyes roam over the bosom of a lady, not his queen. All around him, happy courtiers enjoy themselves. Even the stern Wallachian boyars, who always frown like they're angry and keep to themselves, lighten up a tad and watch Vlad with curious eyes.

My time has come, Vlad thinks. It's time I show them all who I am. I have to show Sigismund that he made the right choice in giving me the title and prove to all the knights and princes that I'll make a better friend than an enemy. And above all, I must show the Wallachians that I'm the man to beat Dan.

Vlad takes a deep breath, and his borrowed breastplate, a bit too small, tightens around his chest. His spurs clang as he steps toward Viscol. He's trained him since he was a foal, but not for this, and the horse's ears twitch with worry as he dances on his feet.

"There we go, Viscol old boy," Vlad whispers as two big men help him up to the saddle since the heavy armor makes it hard to walk, let alone mount a stallion.

Vlad straightens. He touches the dragon's insignia around his neck for good luck, whispers the Lord's prayer, and he's ready.

The trumpets call, and the whole field goes quiet as the herald pronounces the rules of the joust:

"To all shall be known:

"Firstly, we declare that the knights who must joust should run four courses and no more. And if in these courses one knight should hit the other, splintering his lance, the knight whose lance did not break shall be vanquished.

"Furthermore, if one knight splinters two lances and the other only one, the winner shall be the knight who breaks the two lances. But a tie shall be declared if the knight who only splintered one lance knocks off his opponent's helm with his blow.

"If a knight shatters two lances by striking his opponent, and the other knight knocks him off his horse, a tie shall be declared.

"May the best man win."

The herald withdraws to the stalls and leaves the field to the knights.

The custom calls for the squires and younger knights to challenge each other before the experienced champions take their turn, so Vlad waits patiently. But he doesn't have to wait long.

A proud destrier, his shiny coat the color of midnight, charges toward him at full speed like he's chased by the devil. Straight in the saddle, with his long dark hair floating behind him and his fiery eyes full of poison, young Barasab leans over to strike Vlad's shield.

The crowd gasps. The king frowns. A lady faints.

"I challenge you, bastard. I challenge you to a straight honest fight if you even know what that means," Basarab shouts for everyone to hear.

Vlad's hand flies to the hilt of his sword. It's high time to teach this brat a lesson. But he knows better than to cut him here and now. To please the king and obey the rules, he'll have to play the silly game of jousting instead of fighting the real game of war and feeding this insolent kid his tongue like he deserves.

He just wishes he weren't an old man of almost forty with a bad back and achy hands. He wishes he could afford to buy armor instead of borrowing one that doesn't fit. He wishes he had a massive destrier, or at least a warm-blood charger, instead of old Viscol, who's used to hunting and cantering but not to jousting. And he wishes that he had practiced this silly tourney more often, instead of holding a lance for the first time in almost twenty years.

But it is what it is.

Vlad waits for his squire to tighten his breastplate and adjust his écranche, the small square shield attached to his left shoulder that the opponent's lance is meant to strike. When it's done, he leans forward to whisper into Viscol's ear, telling him what a brave boy he is, how he loves him, and that there's nothing to fear, then crosses himself.

CHAPTER 10
THE JOUST

The silence is so deep that Vlad can hear his heart drumming as he leads Viscol to his end of the tilt, the long wooden barrier by which he'll have to charge at full speed to unseat his opponent. And unseat him he must, though he'd much rather kill him.

But these days' tourneys have rules. They're meant to be games, not real fights. The lances are made of blunted soft wood meant to shatter rather than kill, so deaths are rare. They may happen, of course, when someone takes a nasty fall or when there's foul play, and the opponent targets the neck or the horse instead of the écranche strapped to the shoulder. Doing that would get Basarab disqualified and maybe even dishonored, but the kid hates him so much that Vlad wouldn't put it past him to try to kill him. He can only hope. Wouldn't revenge be sweet?

Vlad isn't afraid of death. What he fears is humiliation, and he's had plenty of it.

The king, the nobles, and the whole court have heard this snot-nosed kid insult him again and again, and they saw Vlad do nothing. They don't know how hard it was to keep his temper instead of spilling blood. They don't know him like he is. They only know him as the king's meek, smiling, and always polite errand boy who never loses his temper. Because that's what he wanted them to know.

But if he wants their respect and help, and more than anything, if he wants the throne of Wallachia, it's time to show them who he is. Not an old man with a bad back and too much patience, but blood of the blood and bone of the bone of Mircea the Elder, the man who ruled Wallachia with an iron fist for over thirty years. The man who defeated Bayazid Ilderim. The time has come to channel his father.

Vlad urges Viscol forward toward his starting point. It feels like forever until he reaches his end of the tilt, where his squire awaits to hand him the ten-foot-long, one-and-a-half-inch-thick lance made of soft ash and hollow inside.

Vlad grabs the lance behind the round hand guard and tries it for balance. The thing is tapered, so its long tip is lighter than the handle, but its length alone makes it cumbersome to hold, let alone direct precisely at a gallop. Still, control it he must. The lance's tip must hit Basarab's écranche hard enough to unhorse him or at least shatter. But he can't touch his ugly frog-like helmet or, God forbid, his destrier. That would be a foul and lead to immediate disqualification and endless humiliation.

Vlad tightens his knees around Viscol to turn him parallel to the long barrier and looks for the perfect balance on the lance. He glances at the other end of the tilt where Basarab's angry destrier pummels the frozen earth with his massive hooves. The horse wears a steel chanfron to protect his head, and the caparison on his back showcases an eagle carrying a cross, Wallachia's coat of arms. That gets Vlad's blood to a boil.

It's time.

The trumpet's strident notes break the silence, and Vlad feels Viscol leap forward, taking him to the fight like he knows what this is all about. Vlad tightens his knees and leans forward to keep the force of the impact from unsaddling him. His eyes stay glued to Basarab's écranche, and he struggles to align the lance's tip. Still, the force of his speed turns it so far outward it almost knocks it out of his hand. With all his might, Vlad pulls it back to the center and watches Basarab's lance's tip close in.

The eye-hole in Basarab's frog helmet looks like a nasty grin. The kid screams something, but the blood boiling in Vlad's ears is too loud for him to hear. He only hears the beats of his heart and the drumming of Viscol's hooves as he struggles to align his lance tip with Basarab's guard.

Ten more steps. Eight. Six.

Viscol spooks and leaps to the side. Vlad tightens his knees around him and leans the other way to keep his balance as Basarab's lance whizzes by his ear and the destrier canters to the other end of the tilt.

The trumpets scream.

"The second tilt," the herald says.

Vlad sighs. He leans forward to fondle Viscol's neck and whisper in his ear.

"We can do it, old boy. We can do it. There's nothing to fear; he won't touch you. He won't even touch me if I have anything to say about it. Let's do this, shall we? I can see a carrot in your future. What do you think?"

The horse snorts and stomps his hooves.

"Let's go, then."

Vlad tilts his spear forward, balancing its weight by leaning against the saddle's high back and bending forward to gain flexibility.

Basarab's destrier shakes his head, bares his teeth, and snorts. He rises high on his hind legs, then leaps forward into a canter.

"Time to go, boy," Vlad says.

He tightens his knees around Viscol's belly and touches his long-necked spurs to the horse's flanks, urging him forward. The force of the blow comes from the rider's speed and weight, and Basarab's destrier alone is heavier than Vlad and Viscol combined. They need the advantage of speed.

Viscol leaps forward in soft, fluid leaps, eating up the distance. Basarab's ugly helmet grin comes closer and closer, and the tip of his lance aims straight at Vlad's écranche, growing bigger and bigger. It's almost there when it meets the tip of Vlad's lance and bounces away. The horses canter to the ends of the tilt.

Vlad's back is on fire, and the lance in his hands weighs a ton. He straightens, glad he's still in the saddle, but his strength is waning fast. And Viscol's fading too.

They walk to their end of the field, feeling each other's heartbeats. At the other end, Basarab's grinning helmet defies him, and his black destrier looks enraged.

The trumpet sounds.

"The second sally once more," the herald says.

Vlad sighs and taps Viscol.

"It's now or never, old boy. We don't have another round in us. Let's do it this time, shall we?"

Viscol snorts. Vlad tightens his knees and spurs him forward, praying to God that this time is the last and they won't humiliate themselves. The horse leaps forward.

The wind speeds into Vlad's helmet bringing tears to his eyes and blurring his vision. He squints and blinks, but all he can see of Basarab is a silver blur barreling at him.

Vlad does his best to target what might be Basarab's left shoulder, praying he won't get his helmet, but a gust of wind throws his lance out of balance. Vlad bites his lip, struggling to redirect it, but the long lance is way too heavy. He twists in the saddle, using his whole body strength to bring the lance back in line. It's like pushing a heavy plow through dry dirt, he thinks, remembering working the fields in his childhood. The lance takes a moment, then starts coming around and moves past the midline. Vlad struggles to stop it from turning, but he can't. He's about to get turned around by its weight when he feels something hitting him. He leans back and tightens his legs around his horse, fighting to stay in the saddle.

Shards of wood rain over them, and the crowd erupts in a ruckus. Viscol stops. The sudden loss of speed pushes Vlad forward and keeps him in the saddle.

He tries to balance his lance, but that won't happen. The lance is shattered. All he's got left is the guard and the handle. Vlad glances back to see Basarab splayed on the frozen ground, his helmet askew, and his fiery destrier pummeling the earth near him.

The crowd stands and shouts and erupts into thunderous applause. Sigismund himself claps with a smug smile on his face. The lady by his side throws something at Vlad's feet, holding his eyes for a bit too long. Vlad picks it up and unwraps it. It's a golden buckle of the finest workmanship, a token of appreciation for his bravery. The paper it's wrapped in has just a few words scribbled in Romanian, so smudged they're hard to read.

"Tomorrow at 8 at the Blind Horse Inn."

CHAPTER II
A VERY SECRET MEETING

By the time the tourney was finally over, Vlad's spirit was soaring. His heart burst with the joy of victory, his head swam with plans for the future, and the mulled wine in his belly made them all possible. Wallachia's throne felt closer than ever.

Still, a niggling doubt itched in a corner of his mind. The woman's message said, "Tomorrow at 8 at the Blind Horse Inn," which bothered him no end.

Why the Blind Horse? There were dozens of inns in Nuremberg, most of them dingy places that those who mattered didn't visit unless they weren't keen on being seen. So why the Blind Horse? Was it a coincidence? Or a hint about his other secret meetings?

And what would they want from him? He could only see four options.

The first and most obvious was a lady needing strong loving that her husband couldn't provide. If so, the fair lady who'd thrown him the buckle wouldn't be much of a hardship. But she didn't look like someone who needed to go out of her way to find a lover. The king's eyes rested on her bosom like he didn't mind her himself. So why Vlad?

He could tell himself that his bravery stole her heart, but he was too old to believe it. He'd warmed plenty of beds and succored plenty of women, from ladies to peasants, but he knew he wasn't irresistible. Still, who knows?

The second option was a trap. Basarab didn't take his loss well. He came to Sigismund's court to protect his father's throne, and he failed. First at diplomacy, then again in the tourney. So it was likely that he'd strike again.

The third option was also a trap. What if King Sigismund, may God grant him health and strength, decided to try Vlad and make sure he was trustworthy? What if that invitation was just another sweetened trap?

There was, of course, the fourth option. What if the boyars had finally had enough of Dan and decided to negotiate with Vlad? Wouldn't it be nice if he could grab his father's throne without bloodshed and without selling his soul to pay for an army? That didn't sound likely, but one can hope, can't they?

These pesky thoughts wouldn't leave him alone. He thought about them as he broke his fast with Doamna Cneajna's fresh-baked bread, sausage, and honey. They swirled in his mind as he showed little Mircea how to duel with the new wooden sword he'd carved for him. They were still on his mind when he went to bring Viscol the carrots he'd promised. And ask for advice.

Viscol was the only one Vlad trusted as much as he trusted himself, and his sage advice was the only one Vlad always heeded. Maybe because they never disagreed.

"What do you think, old friend? Should I go?"

Viscol crunched on his carrot and snorted.

"But what if it's a trap?"

Viscol shook his head and pushed him with his nose, asking for another carrot.

"You say it's not, but what if it's another of Basarab's traps? What if I go there to find his hoodlums waiting for me?"

Viscol snorted. Vlad rubbed his forelock and offered him another carrot.

"You're right. He had no time to set it after we threw him in the dust. But what if he did it before?"

Viscol crunched on his carrot with a skeptical look on his long face.

"Right again. The kid didn't think he'd lose, so he wouldn't have prepared that buckle with the message. It has to be something else."

Viscol nodded approvingly and picked up Vlad's last carrot.

"OK then. As you say, only cowards shrink away from knowledge. If I want to know what's what, I'd better go find out."

He thanked the horse and petted him, then went home to get ready. Doamna Cneajna's brow furrowed when she saw him grab his sword and his cloak.

"You're going out? Again? You just won your throne and your tourney. What are you going out for?"

"I have a meeting," Vlad mumbled, rushing out the door to avoid more questions.

He walked the well-known streets to the Blind Horse Inn without hindrance, pushed the door open, and walked in, waiting for trouble. But nobody paid him any mind. Jolly, loud patrons wolfed their sausages and washed them down with beer, keeping an eye on the friendly innkeeper's tired charms.

Vlad chose his old round table in the corner and sat with his back to the wall, as always. He started sipping on his watered-down beer and waited with an eye on the door.

Nothing happened. Lots of nothing until, tired of waiting, Vlad got ready to leave. He signaled the buxom innkeeper, who knew him by now. She smiled and nodded but went the other way. Seconds later, a tall, cloaked figure looking like a Benedictine monk headed Vlad's way. He dragged a heavy chair and sat next to him.

"*Buna seara, prietene,*" he said. "Good evening, my friend." He spoke Romanian, and Vlad's heart tightened. Something about that voice took him to places he hadn't seen in years.

"*Buna seara.*"

"It's good to see you," the man said, dropping his hood to his shoulders. Vlad's heart skipped a beat as long-forgotten memories flooded him.

"Nicolae? Is this really you?"

The man smiled the crooked smile Vlad knew so well. The shaved head was new, but the laughing brown eyes and the white scar across his left brow hadn't changed. Vlad remembered the day he'd gotten it. They'd gone swimming, and Nicolae jumped into the water but found a rock with his face. His mother wasn't pleased.

"No longer. I'm Nijaz now. How are you, old friend?"

Vlad's heart twisted and turned.

"But you used to be Nicolae. Cousin Nicolae. Right?"

Nijaz nodded. "Sure. But that was long ago. How are you these days, Vlad?"

"Never better. I just got my assignment from King Sigismund. I hope to go home to Wallachia before long. How about you?"

"I'm good. It took a lot of learning and plenty of work, but I tore through the ranks of Sultan Murad's army, and these days I'm one of the Grand Vizier's most trusted advisors. So trusted that he sent me here to talk to you."

Vlad looked into his old friend Nicolae's eyes. They were the same, light brown with a touch of honey, just as they were when they fished together, ran from home together, and did all the other things seven-year-old boys do when their mothers aren't watching. But that was ages ago. Now, his old friend was an Ottoman soldier and a high-ranking one at that. How could that be?

"What happened to you?"

Nicolae shrugged. "The old thing. Not long after you left, the sultan's men came to collect boys for devşirme, like they always do. I was the right age and healthy, and I had two younger brothers, so they grabbed me. I screamed and clung to Mother. She cried and begged them to let me go, but they pushed her back and threatened her with their scimitars. She knew she couldn't win, and she had the other kids to look after, so she let me go.

"It was hard. I missed them all for a while, but then I found a new family in my brothers-in-arms. The sultan's janissaries received me with love. I got a roof above my head, all the food I could eat, and lots of training in all things war. I was good enough to fly through the ranks, so these days, I'm Nijaz Pasha, the Grand Vizier's trusted man."

Vlad can't believe this. Can this really be Nicolae, his childhood friend? Or is it just a trap? Is someone going out of their way to ensnare him?

"I missed you and all the things we used to do together. Remember when you fell in the water in our favorite fishing spot, the one behind Popa Ilie's house in the Flowed Lands?"

Nicolae laughed. "You're testing me, aren't you? That was a lousy spot, always windy and muddy. But the corner of the Black River behind the widow's bend, that was our spot."

He's right. Still, Vlad finds it hard to believe that this Nijaz Pasha is his cousin who was like a brother to him. And even if that's true, Vlad should turn him in. His loyalty to the king demands it.

"Why are you here?"

"I came to talk to you. The Grand Vizier trusted me with this mission, thinking that I might be able to speak to your heart. I hope I can. You were my best friend. I spent years mourning your loss, even more than I missed Mother. She had other children, but I only had you. I made other friends. Berat, my friend from Serbia, is a good man. So is Afshin, who came from Greece. We get along and have each other's back. We share a life we didn't choose, but we try to make the most of it. Still, you, Vlad, are my only link to a carefree childhood I'll never get back. I miss you like I'd miss a limb, my friend. I hope you feel it."

Vlad does. The man's words go straight to his heart, making him miss the long-forgotten days of his childhood. But Vlad is no longer a child; he's a man. He knows better than to trust a stranger, even if he used to be a friend.

"What can I do for you, Nicolae? What did they send you here for?"

Nicolae's face darkens, and Vlad feels like he just kicked a puppy. But such is the game of politics. He bites his lip and carries on.

"I'm sorry, old friend, but we both know we no longer are who we used to be. Such is life. So, what can I help you with?"

Nijaz shrugs. "For once, it's the other way 'round. I'm here to tell you that we can help you. I know Sigismund gave you his blessing to be Wallachia's voivode. Good for you. I hope it works out. But don't forget how fickle Sigismund is. That man is as trustworthy as a viper and just as deadly. He'll drop you in the blink of an eye if his interests command it. Don't trust him any further than you can throw him. And when things come to a head, and you need a reliable partner you can trust, give us a sign."

Nicolae takes off a thin rusty ring and drops it on the wooden table. "There. Send this with a safe messenger to the Grand Vizier, and we'll get in touch. Good luck, old friend. I hope to see you again someday."

Najiz stretches his hand over the table. Vlad sighs, wondering how many spies are watching, then shakes his hand.

"Thank you, my friend. I'm glad to see you're well. See you soon, I hope."

"Ins' Allah." The man nods and vanishes into the darkness.

Vlad picks up the ring. It's a coiled snake with a bifurcated tongue, ironically fitted to the circumstances. He knows he should give it to the king.

He slips it on his finger instead.

CHAPTER 12
A YEAR LATER

November 1431, Sighişoara, Transylvania

It's been almost a year, and the witch's prophecies have yet to bear fruit.

Doamna Cneajna is indeed with child again. Her belly is so big she can barely put on her boots, but the throne of Wallachia is still a dream. Further, now that the king has sent them away.

He's been smooth about it like he always is. After all, a man like Sigismund didn't get to be the King of Hungary, Croatia, Bohemia, and the Holy Roman Emperor of Germany for nothing. He knows better than anyone how to keep his friends grateful, even when he gives them the shaft, and how to play his enemies against each other.

A week after the tourney, he took Vlad to the stables to show him the magnificent white stallion that Vladislav, the King of Poland and his perennial rival, had sent him as a gift.

Vlad looked with deep longing at the magnificent snow-white horse who'd half-demolished his stall, bitten two stable boys, and frightened the rest. The horse stared back at Vlad with wicked red eyes. He bared his yellow teeth and neighed something that sounded like a curse. He shook his flowing white mane, snorted, then reared and kicked another hole in the thick stall wall.

Vlad smiled. "He's beautiful and full of life."

"He is, isn't he?" the king said, keeping a safe distance from the crumbling stall and the stallion's strong teeth. "He's a fire-breather, that one. I wonder if Vladislav sent him to me hoping he'd break my neck."

Vlad laughed, but he knew Sigismund wasn't kidding.

"This fire-breather needs a young, strong rider, not an old man like me. That's why I wondered if you'd care to take him off my hands," the king said.

Vlad gasped.

"Me? I'd love to, but I can't afford a horse like that. He must be worth his weight in silver."

Sigismund smiled. "Gold, in fact. But it's a gift. I want to thank you for your faithful service and your patience. I know you're pining for the throne of Wallachia, and I promise you'll have it. Someday. But now is a terrible time. Dan has the boyars on his side, and you know you can't rule Wallachia without them, no matter who supports you. But give him a year or two to step on some toes and overstay his welcome, and the boyars will beg you to take the throne."

"A year or two? But..."

"But what? You're young; you have your whole life ahead of you."

"I'm not young; I'm thirty-nine. In a year or two, I'll be an old man."

"Not old, but wise. An extra year or two will give you time to make friends and cement your alliances. You'll have time to work to secure your throne before getting it. Otherwise, what's the point of taking it just to get chased away? A year or two will give you time to get your stuff in order, strengthen your reputation, and help me."

"Help you?"

"Yes. I need your help in Transylvania. I want you to be Transylvania's military governor and watch my borders in case Dan of Wallachia, or Alexandru of Moldova, your father-in-law, decides to give the Ottomans safe passage to sack my cities and run them through the sword. It's happened before."

"But you have a man in Transylvania. Transylvania's voivode, Ladislaus Csaki, has been there for almost five years, and he's...."

The king shook his head. "Listen, Vlad, there's nothing wrong with Ladislaus. The man is fine, for all he's worth. But I need a man I know I can rely on, and that's you. You're seasoned in battle and know everyone and everything. You speak Hungarian and German better than I do. You even speak Romanian, the language of the peasants, so you can work your connections and your spies and further your interests while looking after mine."

Vlad said yes. What else could he say? The king talked like he asked for a favor, but he was giving an order, and Vlad knew better than to argue a fight he'd already lost.

He went home and told Doamna Cneajna. She paled.

"Transylvania? Are you kidding?"

Vlad shook his head.

"Not at all. But it won't be so bad. As a matter of fact, it's going to be just like home. Most of them speak Romanian. And they're Orthodox like us. And ..."

Doamna Cneajna's eyes caught fire.

"Are you nuts? Just like home? Transylvania is nothing like my home or yours, no matter what language they speak. That country is neither sweet and balmy like Moldova nor tame like your Wallachia. That God-cursed place is nothing but steep mountains, rushing waters, and forbidding forests crawling with strange creatures that aren't what they seem to be. That's where the werewolves and vampires come from, you know? They say that every other Transylvanian bat is a vampire and every other wolf a werewolf. And you can't kill them until you put a silver stake through their heart. As for the witches..."

Vlad shivered, remembering Smaranda, the Transylvanian fortune teller. For some reason, he'd never told Cneajna about her. But it didn't much matter since her prophecies failed to bear fruit.

"That's a myth. All of it. Vampires, werewolves, and witches — none of that is real. They're only meant to keep people out of there. And it works. Look at the Saxon merchants the Hungarian kings brought to reinforce the borders. They've all gotten rich and fat. They don't want competition, so they spread evil rumors to keep everyone away. All that junk is nothing but lies."

Cneajna shook her head. "I don't know, Vlad. My wet nurse was from Transylvania, and she told me that's a harsh, forbidding, and dangerous place. 'Don't go there unless you must,' she said. Are you sure you want your son to grow up there?"

Vlad laughed, but he felt no joy.

"C'mon, woman, show some sense, will you? What do you want me to tell the king? Sorry, but we can't go to Transylvania since my wife is afraid of witches, werewolves, and bats? Could you please just give me my father's throne and let me go to Wallachia instead? Pretty please?"

Doamna Cneajna sighed. "Listen, Vlad. I'll do what I must like I've always done. But you should think again. Be wary. Very wary. And don't forget: If something happens to our son, it will be on you."

Vlad's heart tightened, but he said nothing. What was there to say, after all?

Doamna Cneajna packed their few belongings, and they headed east to Sighişoara, the mighty fortress in the heart of Transylvania, where Vlad had chosen to settle. It took weeks.

Doamna Cneajna grew weary again.

"Why do we need to go all the way to Sighişoara? Why can't we just stop here?" she asked as they got ready to leave again after only two nights to rest the horses. "This place looks fine, and little Mircea is so tired."

Vlad shook his head.

"Sighişoara is where it's at. That burg is a hillside fortress right in the middle of Transylvania, and there's no safer place. They've just rebuilt its three thousand feet of thick defensive walls made of stone and brick that can now withstand even the Ottomans' new cannons. Add the fourteen new battlement-capped donjons the guilds erected, and you'll have a practically impregnable place."

"What guilds?"

"All of them. The rich Saxon guilds that hold the money and the power in all the Transylvanian burgs: the tailors, furriers, jewelers, black-smiths, ropemakers, butchers — all got together and paid to build the donjons that took their name. That gave them pride and made the fortress as safe as can be. There's no safer place for little Mircea to grow up."

So Doamna Cneajna hugged Mircea and did her best to soothe him until they reached their new home, a square yellow house near the Councilmen's Tower in Sighişoara's Main Square. Like the merchants' houses surrounding it, it's a massive, three-story stone building with a sharp tiled roof to shake off the snow and tiny windows to keep out the riffraff. The main entrance is on the ground floor, through the quarters of Vlad's garrison, and the other two are on the next level, where a narrow stairway leads to their quarters.

Vlad is just heading upstairs when he hears a bloodcurdling scream.

CHAPTER 13
WOMEN'S BUSINESS

Vlad's hand finds the hilt of his sword. He flies up the steep stairs three at a time, blasts open the door, and pulls out his blade.

Frau Helga, the housekeeper, jumps back and drops the cup she's holding. The wine spills on the wooden floor, thick and red like blood.

"What happened?" Vlad asks, just as another otherworldly scream shakes the walls. "What was that?"

Frau Helga sighs with relief.

"Oh, *Mein Gott,* you almost killed me. I thought something terrible had happened. That's Doamna Cneajna. Her time has come."

"Her time? What time?"

Frau Helga looks at Vlad like he's feeble.

"Your lady is in labor. Your baby is about to be born."

"Now? I thought she had a few more weeks," Vlad says, sliding his sword back into its scabbard and feeling stupid.

Frau Helga shrugs.

"Babies come when they choose to. It looks like this one chose to come early."

"How's she doing?"

"She's doing fine. The midwife sent me for a cup of wine to dull the pain. I guess I'll get another," she says, looking at the wine on the floor.

"I'm sorry, Frau Helga," Vlad mumbles as he opens the door to Doamna Cneajna's room.

The heat and the smell of human bodies hit him like a punch. The small bedroom is standing-room only, and the dozen or so women fussing around Doamna Cneajna glare at him like he's an intruder. And he is. Men aren't supposed to witness the birth of their children. They should be out and about, hunting, whoring, or fighting while their wives go through labor. Men should only return when the women are done. But Vlad is Transylvania's military governor, and as such, he has the power of life and death over every soul in the room. So they don't say anything. They just look at him down their noses and wait.

"How is she doing?" Vlad asks nobody in particular.

The midwife, a small gray-haired woman dressed in black with blue eyes sharper than the steel of Vlad's dagger, looks up from between Cneajna's legs.

"She's fine. The baby's right here; she just needs to push harder."

Vlad squeezes through the crowd to reach Cneajna's hand and lifts it to his lips.

"I have faith in you, my lady. Give me a son," he says.

Doamna Cneajna sighs. Her dark-circled eyes look like holes in her pale face glowing with sweat. She nods, then opens her mouth and lets out another terrible scream as a wave of pain rips through her. Vlad dashes out without looking back.

CHAPTER 14
VLAD DRACULA

It's been hours since Vlad went downstairs to the garrison. The soldiers offered him wine to soften the wait. They rose their cups to Doamna Cneajna's health, to a healthy baby boy, to King Sigismund, then to the throne of Wallachia. By the time the midwife comes to fetch him, they've had quite a few.

"All done. Come meet your new son," she says.

Vlad's heart melts.

"How is he?"

"He's a strong boy with a head full of black hair. And he's hungry already," she pants, chasing Vlad up the stairs.

Vlad's heart melts with gratitude. For the midwife, even though she'll be well rewarded since she delivered a baby boy; for his wife, who tore herself apart to give him a son; and for the Good God, who made it all happen. He runs up the stairs and opens the door to Cneajna's bedroom.

Thank God, the women are all gone but one. His wife's asleep, her face whiter than snow. The woman smiles and presents him with a red-faced, screaming bundle.

"This is your son. What shall he be named?"

Vlad thinks. His eldest son is Mircea, after Mircea the Elder, his father. But this one...

"His name is Vlad. He'll be Vlad Dracula, Vlad Dracul's son."

He contemplates the little red face scrunched in anger. The baby's lips quiver, searching for something he can't find. He shrieks, twists, and shrieks again.

Vlad hands him back to the woman.

"What does he want?"

The woman laughs.

"He needs a breast."

"So go on and give it to him," Vlad says. The woman blushes and looks away.

The midwife shakes her head.

"She can't. She's not a wet nurse. And that's the problem, my lord."

"What problem?"

"Your wife interviewed a dozen women expecting to give birth soon. But her baby came early, and none of the women has birthed yet. So, we don't have a wet nurse."

Vlad shrugs. "What do you want me to do? Go find another. Or get him a goat or a sheep."

The midwife shakes her head. "That, we can do. But the young prince would do much better with a healthy woman's milk. He'd grow healthier and stronger. Plus, a wet nurse would take care of the baby, allowing your wife to look after your home, yourself, and your older son. I highly recommend that."

Vlad shrugs. "Get one, then."

The woman sighs. "There's this girl..."

"Girl?"

"She had a baby, but then he disappeared, and the poor girl went crazy with pain. She's still frantic and out of sorts, but her breasts are full of milk, and she needs a soul to hold..."

Vlad shrugs. "Get her then. My wife will decide when she's ready. What's her name?"

"Her name is Luna."

CHAPTER 15

THE BAT

It's been almost a year since Luna came into their lives, and she's been everything the midwife said and then some, Vlad Dracul thinks, standing in the nursery door to watch little Vlad take his first unsteady steps. Luna's arms hold him lovingly as his impatient little feet wrapped in sheepskin booties drum the worn wooden floors of the nursery. Her narrow dark eyes stay glued to him. What a strange girl! She rarely speaks, and then only in whispers, and she glides through the house with the silent drift of a ghost.

But Vlad stopped screaming the moment she touched him. When his greedy little mouth found her breast, Luna smiled, and her sharp face glowed with beauty.

She held him to her breast and sang to him in a strange language that no one understood. Vlad's curious green eyes never left her face as she whispered and played with him. She even slept on a straw mattress by his cradle.

Doamna Cneajna didn't like her much. "She's a strange girl," she said when she finally felt well enough to hold her baby. "I liked the other women better."

Vlad Dracul shrugged. "Get one of them, then, and send her away."

Doamna Cneajna did. But the moment Luna handed Vlad to the new wet nurse Doamna had chosen, Vlad started screaming and wouldn't stop. He shrieked and cried until he turned purple, kicking his tiny feet and scrunching his narrow face in powerless anger.

The new wet nurse sang him lullabies, rocked him, and offered him her breast, but the baby turned away as if it were hot and screamed even louder.

She changed his diapers and bathed him with lukewarm water infused with rosemary and lavender to ward off the evil eye, but the baby kept screaming.

She made chamomile tea sweetened with acacia bee honey to soothe his stomach. Vlad puked it out.

She sliced red onion, marinated it in warm wine vinegar, then tied it in a poultice around his belly to ward off colic. The baby screamed as if she'd set him on fire.

She soaked a clean cloth in sweet wine and put it in his mouth. He spat it out.

Vlad Dracul couldn't take it anymore. He grabbed a blanket and went to sleep down in the garrison with the soldiers, and took Dragon, the fire-breathing stallion the king had given him, on a long canter hoping to cool his mind. But Doamna Cneajna had nowhere to go.

After three days and two nights, she gave up.

"Bring Luna back."

The moment Luna touched him, Vlad went quiet. His furrowed brow softened, his tiny hands cupped her breast, and he fell asleep. That was last year, and Luna never left again.

Thank God, Vlad Dracul thinks, watching Vlad's happy smile. She may be weird, but the kid's healthy and happy. Doamna Cneajna had better get used to her.

"People talk," she said only last night over dinner.

Vlad took out his dagger and stabbed a golden link of fried sausage perfumed with garlic and oregano. He set it on his thick bread trencher on top of the stewed cabbage, and took a thirsty sip of wine, wondering if she'd already heard about the girl in Boiu he'd visited the week before.

"About what?" he asked.

"About how weird Luna is. She never talks to anyone, and she never leaves the house till dark, even in winter. It's like she hates the sun."

Vlad Dracul sighed with relief. "Maybe she does. Or maybe she's too busy looking after Vlad to have time for anything else until he's asleep. What's it to you?"

"He's... he's so attached to her, it's not normal. It's like he's hers, not mine."

"He's just a baby, not yet one year old. She's with him all the time while you look after the house and Mircea and care for the church and the poor, like the governor's wife should. You barely ever spend time with him."

"But I'm his mother!"

Vlad shrugged and emptied his cup. Good wine, this one, from Jidvei. Crisp and smooth, with a hint of almonds and peaches.

"He doesn't know it yet. But he will," he said.

Women! Instead of being happy that the baby's healthy and well looked after, she's jealous that he loves Luna more than her. They always want what they can't have. Thank God she doesn't know about the girl in Boiu...

Still, there's some truth to her words. Luna is strange, sometimes downright weird. Like that night when he thought he'd heard an odd fluttering sound coming from little Vlad's room. He stepped in to check and found the baby alone but for a bat on the windowsill. Vlad rushed to get his sword, but by the time he returned, Luna was back, and the bat was gone.

"Where were you?" he asked.

"Just...doing my business," she said. Still, something felt off.

Then there was that time Vlad thought he saw blood on the baby's lips. He'd asked Luna, and she explained that the baby was teething, and he chewed on her nipples. Vlad Dracul didn't push it. He didn't tell Cneajna, who was already riled enough against the girl. Still, every now and then, he wondered whether...

"Governor?"

Vlad turned to the soldier.

"There's a message from Wallachia."

A tired man covered in dust handed him a scroll. Vlad took it and checked the red wax seal. It bore the sign of Spătar Stanciu, one of his few allies at Dan's court, and it was intact.

He broke it and read: "Your half-brother Alexandru Aldea ousted Dan, who ran away and is now believed dead. Alexandru took the throne without a fight with help from King Sigismund."

CHAPTER 16

GO GET AN ARMY!

Vlad saddled Dragon and took him for a hard canter like he always does when his soul is in turmoil. Fighting the fiery stallion releases the worst of his anger, so it doesn't cloud his judgment, and stops him from snapping at those he swore to protect. It took him a while, but Vlad finally learned to control his temper and not mistreat innocent people like he sometimes did when he was young.

He cantered up and down the frozen hills around Sighișoara until Dragon's fire went out. The stallion hung his head and stopped fighting him.

Then, and only then, Vlad headed back home at a trot.

By the time he gets back in town, his rage is finally spent, but his head isn't any clearer. He wishes he knew what to do.

The one thing he's lived for, the throne of Wallachia, is gone.

He's been dreaming about it ever since he was a young child in Cobia, a village near Târgoviște, where he lived with his mother. She told him that his father, a man he'd never met, was the voivode of Wallachia, the most powerful man in the country.

"He rides a big horse and has more cows and sheep than he can count."

"Where does he live?" Vlad had asked.

"At the Royal Court of Târgoviște, which is even bigger than the village church. Your father has the power of life and death over everyone in the country. He sits on a carved throne to give justice to the people, and everyone listens to him. If you're a good boy and work very hard, one day, maybe, you could sit on that throne too. God willing."

"Can I ride a horse, too?" he'd asked.

She'd laughed and said yes.

The hope for the throne — and the horse — kept him going when the father he'd never met took him away from his home and his mother and dropped him at Sigismund's court, telling him to be good and make him proud if he wanted to sit on the throne.

Later on, the hope for that throne kept him wandering from Buda to Prague, Byzantium, and Genoa to lend his sword to wars that weren't his and look for a wife to strengthen his claim. That's how he chose Cneajna. And that's why he went back to Sigismund and swore him fealty.

But now, his hope for the throne of Wallachia has turned to dust. Sigismund, his friend, the man he swore to support and protect, stabbed him in the back. He sent him here to goddamn Transylvania to get rid of him, then gave his throne to Alexandru, his bitter enemy.

Vlad stumbles on his words telling Cneajna, praying she won't fall apart like she does every time the roast burns or Mircea's late for dinner after playing with the neighbors' sons. Today, he doesn't have what it takes to be patient.

But it turns out that he doesn't need to. Doamna Cneajna sits quietly by the window, listening to his every word with her eyes glued to the shirt she embroiders. She shows no emotion other than the trembling of the needle coming in and out of the white linen. When he's done, she looks up.

"So, what will you do?"

Vlad shrugs.

"I don't know. But I think we should flee to Poland. King Vladislav and I go way back. We fought together many times. And we're friends. Maybe he could..."

"He could what?"

"He could help us?"

"How?"

"I could get a position in his army. These damn wars never end, so they always need reliable, experienced officers, and I've been through more fights than I can count. We'd have a roof above our heads and the boys..."

"The boys?"

"The boys could go into the military when they get old enough. They'd have a career."

"Are you crazy?"

Doamna Cneajna throws her embroidery and stands to pace. Her hands are fisted on her hips, her cheeks burn, and her eyes sparkle. Vlad hasn't seen her so mad since the day she learned about that girl in Biertan.

"You want the boys to leave the only home they know, and you'll leave your position as the military governor of Transylvania, the highest man here but for the voivode, to do what? Beg for a job in the Polish army? You've got to be kidding me!"

Vlad Dracul gasps. "But...the king betrayed me."

"The king did what kings do. Whatever they want. He chose to support your half-brother instead of you. For now. You should wonder why."

Vlad shakes his head.

"It doesn't matter why. Sigismund promised me the throne. He even handed me the Staff of Office, then sent me here to linger and gave my throne to Alexandru. What difference does it make what he did it for? Facts are facts."

"Sure they are. And feelings are feelings, and they don't play together well. You know what you're feeling?"

"Anger. And injustice."

"True enough. Just like I did when I heard that that girl in Biertan was with child. And the others. While I'm your wife. I keep your house, I rear your children, and I uphold your image as the governor of Transylvania in this God-forsaken frozen place. I was so angry I could have killed you. But I didn't. You know why?"

Vlad stares at his wife. She's no longer the meek, obedient woman he's had for years. This one's a harpy, and there's no doubt she could kill.

"I don't."

"Because of the children. This isn't about me being stilted as you sneak around to bed other women. Nor about you getting the shaft as Sigismund lies to you and gives the throne to your brother. This is about Mircea and little Vlad. They have a blood-right to the throne of Wallachia. Will you take that away from them?"

Vlad sighs.

"What do you want me to do?"

"I want you to think about them. Work for them. Suffer for them, like I do. Swallow your jealousy, your anger, and your spite to preserve the God-given right of your sons. They're bone of the bone of Alexandru cel Bun and Mircea the Elder. No contender to the Wallachian throne has better blood flowing through his veins, not even you. Make that matter. Give them their chance."

"But how?"

"Stay put. We're safe here. We have a roof over our heads, and you have a position that allows you to build our kids' futures. Swallow your spite and thank Sigismund for his trust. I know it tastes bitter. So what? I was bitter when I sent a birth gift to your whore; thank God she had a girl, not a boy to fight mine for the throne. But we do what we must to smooth our children's path. Sooner or later, the king will get tired of Alexandru. The boyars too. That Wallachian throne is a nest of thorns. As long as you hold it, everyone wants you dead, even your brothers. And there's no keeping it. How many reigns have they had since Mircea the Elder died?"

"Father died in January 1418. Since that, they've had…" Vlad starts counting on his fingers, then starts over. Doamna Cneajna's hard eyes weighing on him don't help any.

"They've had five princes and eighteen reigns. Or so. Some were no longer than a few weeks," he says.

"So what? A few days on that throne is all it takes to make our boys the sons of a voivode and strengthen their claim. And, while Alexandru is busy making enemies and Sigismund gets tired of him, you'll get ready. My father died, God rest his soul, so he can't help us, but Ilias, my brother, will, as long as he sits on Moldova's throne. While the boyars get fed up with Alexandru, you go get an army."

Vlad stares at Cneajna like he's never seen her. Where did the shy girl he married go? And who's this fire-breathing woman by his side?

"The mother of your sons will help you get the throne," Smaranda had said. She was right.

CHAPTER 17

1 WANT TO SEE THE HANGING

That was three years ago, and they were well-spent years. While waiting for Alexandru Aldea to overstay his welcome, Vlad worked hard to make allies and gathered an army. He criss-crossed Transylvania and courted the Saxon burgs of Sibiu and Kronstadt for support.

"Know ye," he wrote to the Kronstadt burgomaster, "that my Master and Emperor entrusted me with the protection of this region, and pray do not make peace with my enemies in Wallachia without my consent."

And, since he was the king's trusted man and friend, they listened. Even more so after Sigismund allowed him to mint his own coin with the Dragon's effigy on one side and the princely eagle of Wallachia on the other. Vlad's golden ducats became legal tender all over Transylvania and Hungary. That allowed him to buy armor and weapons for his volunteers from the duchies of Amlas and Făgăraș, the traditional fief of Wallachian princes that Sigismund had put under his power.

Last year, just like Doamna Cneajna had predicted, Sigismund got tired of Alexandru playing footsie with the Ottomans. Whether to warn

Alexandru or to repay Vlad Dracul for his faithful service, Sigismund listened to the Teutonic Order's grand master and let Vlad gather an army and buy weapons.

Vlad even bought some of the new cannons. Those God-awful heavy, stinky tools of the devil can crush an armored knight on his horse from a hundred feet away like a dog crushes a flea between its teeth. Their God-cursed projectiles can break walls and crumble towers hundreds of feet away, even across moats and rivers, making long castle sieges a thing of the past.

In the meantime, Doamna Cneajna kept his house and upheld Vlad Dracul's reputation as a man of the faith, generous to churches, and kind to the poor. And she's seen to the boys' education, preparing them to be princes.

And what a good job she did, Vlad thinks, watching his sons gallop home on the narrow cobblestoned street. Their eyes shine with the joy of the race as they ride bareback on their nimble ponies. Mircea's first, like he should be, since he's almost eight, but Vlad is not far behind, though he's barely four.

"I won, even though you cheated. You weren't supposed to take that shortcut," Mircea says, jumping off his steamy horse.

"What's cheated?" little Vlad asks.

Vlad Dracul helps him down.

"That's when you don't play by the rules."

"Sure I do. Just not by his rules," Vlad says, pointing his sharp chin at his brother. "I make my rules."

Vlad Dracul laughs.

"What did you boys do today?"

"We went to the pond with Hans and Gyula. We hunted crows with our slingshots. And we fished, but I didn't catch anything," Vlad says.

"Of course you didn't. I told you not to kill the worms before you hook them, but you never listen," Mircea says.

Vlad shrugs.

"You didn't catch anything either."

"But I..."

Vlad Dracul shakes his head.

"That's enough. Let's go upstairs. Your mother is waiting for us with dinner."

They follow him upstairs to the warm kitchen that smells like freshly baked bread and rabbit braised with white wine and thyme. The shiny wooden table, long enough for a dozen, is loaded with heavy black pots steaming mouthwatering aromas. There's a golden round bread as big as a cart's wheel, wooden plates loaded with fresh white sheep's cheese, juicy red apples, and a pot of golden honey. There's way too much food for the four of them, but whatever's left will feed the orphans and the widows at the St. Nicholas Church and enhance Vlad Dracul's reputation as a man of God.

Doamna Cneajna wipes her sweaty forehead with her sleeve. Her tired narrow face makes her belly look even bigger as she bends to hug Mircea.

"Where's Vlad?"

Mircea shrugs. "He must have stopped by his room to watch the criminals being taken to the Jeweler's Donjon for the hanging."

Doamna Cneajna frowns. "I don't understand why he loves to do that."

"I'll get him," Vlad Dracul says.

He takes the steps one floor down to Vlad's bedroom to find him glued to the window. The child's green eyes shine as he watches the long string of men in rags stumble across the city square, their chains clanging along the cobblestones.

Vlad Dracul puts his hand on his son's shoulder.

"What are you watching?"

"The men."

"Why?"

Little Vlad shrugs.

"You like them?"

"No."

"So why are you watching them, then?"

"I don't know."

"You know that those are bad people who did terrible things. They're killers, thieves, and rapists who hurt other people, and it's their time to pay for their terrible deeds."

"Pay how?"

"They'll pay with their life, so they never hurt anyone again. Even more, they'll set an example for all those who may think they can get away with breaking the law. All those who see them hang will think twice before doing the same. That's the king's law, and it's a good law. And, as Transylvania's governor, it's my job to see that it's applied fairly."

A shiver goes through Vlad's little body.

He's scared, Vlad Dracul thinks. Of course, he is. My bad. He's just a child, way too young to learn about killing, raping, and hanging.

"Don't be afraid, little one. I'm here to protect you."

"I'm not afraid."

"What are you then?"

"I'm...Father, can I go watch the hanging?"

CHAPTER 18
NO BAT

Once dinner's over and the kids go to sleep, Doamna Cneajna sits on her bed. She bends over to take off her shoes, but her belly gets in the way. She groans, pushes them off, squeezes under the covers, and sighs with relief when she finds the hot bricks the servants put in the bed to warm it up.

"How are you feeling?" Vlad Dracul asks.

"Tired. So tired."

"No wonder, with everything you do. And you're so heavy. But just another week or two, and…"

Doamna Cneajna laughs. "You think it gets easier? Think again. It doesn't get any easier when they come out. Those two are plenty of work already. Having a baby to feed and look after…"

"Are you kidding? You can't do it all by yourself! And why should you? Get a wet nurse!"

Doamna Cneajna shrugs. "I don't know. After the last one…."

It's been more than a year since Luna disappeared, but that's not something they ever talk about. It took little Vlad forever to get over her absence. At first, he wouldn't eat and cried himself to sleep every night. Now it looks like he's forgotten her. But truth be told, he hasn't been the same since she left. Vlad can't remember him laughing or even smiling since Luna disappeared.

"What do you think happened to her?" Doamna Cneajna whispers.

Vlad shrugs. "I don't know. Maybe she found a better offer and went somewhere else."

Doamna Cneajna glances at Vlad like he's nuts.

"You don't really believe that, do you?"

Vlad sighs. "I don't know what I believe. I find it hard to believe that Luna could leave Vlad without looking back. I've never seen someone more devoted to a child that wasn't hers. But what else could have happened?"

"What if something happened to her? What if someone did something to her?"

"Here, in a house full of soldiers?"

"Maybe not here. You know how she liked to roam at night."

Vlad shrugs. "I had the men scour the whole fortress of Sighișoara and every village within twenty miles. We looked for her all over the forests, inside wells, and by the rivers. Everywhere. We never found a trace of her. If she was killed, we'd have found her."

"Maybe." Doamna Cneajna's voice is heavy with doubt.

"What are you thinking?"

"I'm thinking this isn't like my Moldova, where the sun shines most days of the year, the sky is blue, and things are just what they seem to be. Not even your Wallachia, with its golden wheat fields and misty marshes. This is Transylvania, the land between the forests, where vampires, werewolves, strigoi, and witches roam the woods. And God knows what other otherworldly creatures.

Vlad remembers the night he found a bat in Vlad's room, and he shivers. He went to get a weapon and returned to find Luna instead. But how does that make any sense?

"You know about the bat?" Doamna Cneajna whispers as if she heard his thoughts.

"What bat?"

"The night Luna disappeared, the gardener shot a bat. He said it was heading to Vlad's open window. He got him with one arrow, then stabbed him with a silver dagger to be extra sure. They say half of these bats are vampires, and the only way to kill them is to run a silver stake through their heart."

"That's nothing but ignorant peasant superstition," Vlad said, trying to convince himself first. "You shouldn't listen to this nonsense."

"Maybe. I don't know. Luna never liked garlic. She didn't much like the sun, either."

"So, what happened to the bat?"

"He buried it."

"Where?"

"I don't know."

Vlad couldn't sleep that night. He went to find the gardener at the crack of dawn.

"Where did you bury that bat last year?"

"Under the lilac tree by the church."

"Let's find it."

They dug and dug but found nothing, not even the bones. The bat was gone.

CHAPTER 19

A DAY IN THE COUNTRY

A week passed, then another.

The sun wasn't up yet when a bloodcurdling scream woke Vlad from a fitful sleep in which he was fighting Basarab. He reached for his sword before he realized it was Doamna Cneajna, whose time had come.

Time to go, Vlad thought. The women who'll help her in labor don't want him here any more than he wants to be in their way. He headed to the door.

"Vlad?" Doamna Cneajna's voice cracked with pain.

"Yes?"

"Take the boys."

Oops. He hadn't counted on that. He thought he'd go down to inspect the garrison and then take a long canter to clear his head, but the boys?

Doamna Cneajna read the doubt in his eyes.

"If this isn't something for you to watch, you think they should?"

Vlad Dracul sighed. He woke up the boys and took them to the stables.

"Where are we going?" Mircea asked.

I'd be damned if I knew. Anywhere but home, Vlad Dracul thought, but didn't say it.

"We're going to have an all-boys day. The three of us will inspect the land and learn about the country."

He pushed old Viscol into a light canter, but the boys passed him at a gallop. First Mircea, his windswept black curls slapping his face, and then Vlad, his green eyes sparkling, his narrow face flushed with excitement.

Vlad Dracul followed them up the steep hills, over the frosty pastures, all the way to the top where a late fall morning sun poured gold over the brown grass and warmed the few leaves still clinging to the trees. He stopped with the sun at his back, looking down over the mighty fortress of Sighișoara. From up here, the town looked like a nativity scene.

The red-tiled roofs, built sharp to shed the snow, stuck close to each other while trying to stand out, like a bunch of peasant girls in their best Sunday clothes gathered for a dance. Blue smoke rose straight up from skinny chimneys. Standing alone on top of Church Hill, the old white church with its sharp triangular roof kept an eye on the houses at the foot of the hill. Down to the right, the Council Tower stood head and shoulders above all other buildings like a queen bee above the worker bees crowding each other.

The hills hugged the city like a pair of hands cupped to hold something precious. Far beyond, the white-crowned steep peaks of the Carpathians stood out against the clear blue sky.

"Isn't it beautiful?" Vlad Dracul asks. "The houses, the churches, and those white mountains far behind?"

Mircea nods. Little Vlad sniffs.

"Is this all ours?"

"It's ours to look after. For now."

"And then?"

Vlad Dracul sighs. "God willing, one day, we'll head south to Wallachia. That's our country, where my father and your grandfather, Mircea the Elder, used to be voivode."

"When?" Mircea asks.

"Someday soon. When the time will be right."

"I want to go now," little Vlad says.

Vlad Dracul ruffles his hair.

"Not yet. But one day, we will. We'll head back and take my father's throne. I'll be the voivode; then you, Mircea, will be voivode after me; and then you, Vlad, will follow."

"I don't want to follow. I want to go first," Vlad says, his green eyes bright with fury.

Vlad laughs.

"You can't. I go first, then Mircea. You're too young."

"I'm not young. Mother said I'm almost five."

"That's young."

"But I was younger before. And I don't want to be the youngest. I want to be older."

"Well, come to think of that, I have good news for you."

"What?"

"You're going to be an older brother."

"Older than Mircea?"

"No. Older than your new brother. Or sister. Your mother will have another baby."

"When?"

"She's having it now. We'll meet it when we go home."

Vlad's brows furrowed.

"I don't want a baby. I want a horse."

"You have a horse."

"I want a bigger horse."

"Why don't you want a baby?"

"Because... Will Luna come back to feed it?

Vlad sighed.

"I don't think so. I think your mother will find another woman to look after the baby."

"Why not Luna?"

"I...we don't know where she is."

"But if you did, would you bring her back?"

"I don't know. That's for your mother to decide."

"Then, if I can't have Luna, I don't want the baby."

Vlad sighed again, wondering what to say. This wasn't going anywhere good.

Mircea shook his head.

"You don't have a choice, you stupid. The baby will be there whether you like it or not, and you'll have to put up with it just like I put up with you."

"No, I won't."

"Really? So what are you going to do?"

"I'll kill it."

CHAPTER 20

RADU THE HANDSOME

Childish words, Vlad Dracul thought. No need to worry Doamna Cneajna about them. She's got enough on her plate already.

By the time they get home that evening, he's already forgotten.

Doamna Cneajna's labor is done. Her face is tired, but she glows with love and pride like a Madonna as she presents Vlad with the fruit of her labors.

Vlad hugs her and holds the new baby. It's another boy, just like that witch in Nuremberg promised, and Vlad's heart melts with love as he gazes in his new son's eyes.

But this one is not like the others. Unlike Mircea and Vlad who are dark-haired, green-eyed, and full of fire, like him, this baby takes after his mother. He's blond, blue-eyed, and looks like he's made of sun rays and honey.

"He's the most beautiful baby I've ever seen," the midwife says, gazing into the round eyes the color of forget-me-nots that wonder at the world.

"He is, isn't he? Just like his father," says the new wet nurse.

Vlad gives her a once-over. She's nothing like Luna. This one is pink and soft, with dimples in her cheeks and slippery eyes that look at Vlad like she doesn't mind him.

He wouln't mind her either, but Doamna Cneajna's right here, though she's too tired to notice. But her wrath is something to behold, and Vlad doesn't need it one bit.

"What's his name?" the woman asks.

"His name is Radu, after Radu the Black, my forefather and Wallachia's founder," Vlad says.

The woman laughs. "Well, this one ain't black. This one's gonna be Radu the Handsome."

The baby smiles like he agrees, and Vlad Dracul's heart twists with love. This is the third son his wife has given him, let alone the other one or two he fathered elsewhere. His line is now secure. All he needs is a throne.

He sits by Doamna Cneajna and kisses her hand. Her face is pale and drawn, but the happiness in her eyes makes her beautiful.

"Thank you, my lady, for our son. He's as beautiful as you, and he's healthy. He'll make a great voivode someday, should God wish it."

Doamna Cneajna's eyes widen. "You've heard something?"

"I just got a message from Wallachia. Alexandru fell ill. He went to Istanbul to be cared for by Sultan Murad's own doctor and left Boyar Albu to look after the country."

"What will you do?" Cneajna whispers.

"It's time I went. I've sent word to my men in Amlas and Făgăraș to get ready, and I wrote to Sigismund to ask for permission. As soon as I get it, I'll be on my way.

"How long will you be gone?"

"God only knows. As long as it takes. But I know that you'll look after our house and our boys while I'm gone. I'll send for you all as soon as I take the throne."

"Soon, I hope."

"God willing."

Vlad leans over to kiss her forehead, when a loud ruckus erupts in the street. Men scream, weapons clang, children cry. The women in the room huddle together.

Vlad grabs his sword and runs downstairs.

Two of his soldiers hold a young man, hardly more than a child. His clothes are in tatters, and his eyes shine with tears.

Ten feet away, little Vlad leans against the house, holding his bow. His little red face is stained with tears. In the middle of the cobblestoned street, a spotted dog lays in a pool of blood, heaving his last breaths around the arrow skewering him.

"What happened?" Vlad Dracul asks.

"This man struck the prince," a soldier says.

"He killed my dog. He shot him with an arrow and killed him. Look at him," the young man shouts. He struggles to break free, but the soldiers hold him tight.

Vlad Dracul turns to his son. "Are you OK?"

Little Vlad stomps his feet. "He hit me. He dared to hit me."

Vlad looks him up and down but sees nothing amiss other than the red mark on his cheek. He tries to hug and comfort him, but little Vlad wants none of it. He screams in a fit of rage, and Vlad Dracul lets him be.

He turns to the soldiers and points to the young man. "Take him."

The soldiers drag the man to the tower where the hangings are done.

CHAPTER 21

THE CURSE OF THE DRACULAS

It took hours for little Vlad to settle. He sobbed even in his sleep, his little face scrunched in anger.

"He's had a hard day," Doamna Cneajna said, wrapping Vlad's blue woolen blanket around him. "Getting a new brother and being struck by a peasant, all in one day, it's more than a little boy's heart can handle."

Vlad sighed.

"I wish he didn't kill the dog, though. We have enough enemies; we don't need the locals hating on us. Especially not now, when I'm about to leave you here alone with the children."

But it didn't take that long.

Two mornings later, they were breaking their fast. Vlad Dracul sat at the head of the table, cutting thick trenchers out of the warm round bread. Mircea took one and smeared on it a thick layer of yellow butter. He added a spoonful of gooey apricot jam flavored with their own crushed seeds, then bit into it.

Little Vlad grabbed a piece of dry sausage and sliced it with his dagger when someone knocked at the door.

"Governor? There's a woman here to see you."

Vlad Dracul's heart jumped. A woman? The girl in Boiu? Or one of the others?

"I'll see her outside," he said, but it was too late. The door opened, and an old woman in tattered clothes broke into the room.

She dropped to her knees and joined her hands in prayer.

"Please, governor. My grandson is all I have. He's the light of my eyes and my only help. The black death took his parents and his sister when he was just a baby. I brought him up, and he's everything I have. Please let him go."

Her pale eyes begged Vlad Dracul.

"Who are you? And who's your grandson?"

"The boy you sent to jail the other day. Please, governor. He's only thirteen. He didn't know what he was doing. Please forgive him. He got crazy with anger when your son killed his dog. He brought it up from a pup and loved him with all his heart. Please let him go."

Vlad sighed.

"I can't. Your boy struck my son, a prince of Wallachia. I can't let him go."

"Please, governor. He's just a child. He won't ever do it again. I'll take him with me, and we'll go..."

"Listen, woman, I can't. If I allow any peasant to hit my son, the blood of my blood, the royal bone of Wallachia, without punishment, what will happen next? What will the next hot-headed peasant do, knowing nothing happened to your grandson? I shudder to think."

The woman crawled on her knees and touched her forehead to the floor.

"Please, governor. I'll..."

"There's nothing you can do, woman. Nothing. You should have taught him better."

He turned to the soldiers in the door.

"Take her."

The men pulled her to her feet.

"Let's go, woman."

The woman laughed a bone-chilling laugh.

Little Vlad looked up. Mircea gasped. Doamna Cneajna blanched.

That otherworldly, terrible laugh froze Vlad Dracul's heart.

"You say there's nothing you can do? But I can. And I will."

Her pale eyes glowed as if she were possessed, and her gnarled hands with long, claw-like finger nails pointed at Vlad.

"I curse you, Vlad Dracul. From the broken heart of a mother and grandmother that God will listen to, I curse you. I curse you and your sons and their unborn sons from the first to the last. I curse your sons to hate each other. And I curse you to lose them all. They'll be taken from your side, and you'll die without ever seeing them again. All but one. Your oldest."

"That one, your heir, you'll live to watch him die. He'll die a death like you wouldn't wish on your worst enemy. You'll see it all, and only after that you'll die. Broken, betrayed, and alone."

Her skull-like face turned to little Vlad.

"As for you, blood-lusting young devil, I curse you to be forever alone. Just like me, you will lose everyone and everything you love. Everything. I curse you to hold onto nobody, ever. Your whole life will be nothing but hate, blood, and sorrow."

Empty of words, Vlad Dracul signaled the soldiers to take her. They dragged her out, but she kept screaming.

"I curse you all, from now and until the last generation of the House of Basarab. Your house will die because of you!"

Paler than snow, Doamna Cneajna held on to the table. Mircea's eyes glittered with tears. Vlad Dracul's heart froze.

Little Vlad took another bite from his sausage.

CHAPTER 22
GOING TO WAR

Sighişoara 1436

The following months weren't easy. The old woman's curse weighed on their hearts and hung above their heads like a storm-heavy sky. For weeks, they lived in fear, waiting for God's wrath to manifest. All but little Vlad, who was too young to understand.

But nothing happened. Nothing bad, that is. Little Radu grew handsome and healthy, and the celebration of his baptism was glorious. His brother Mircea, who was his godfather, held him in front of the altar and renounced Satan and all evil in his name, cleaning him of the original sin and setting him straight with God.

Everyone agreed that it was a beautiful ceremony. Even better, the baptismal church didn't catch fire this time like the one after Vlad's baptism. That time, the whole church had burned into the ground: the holy altar, the blessed icon of the Virgin, and even the holy relic of St. Nicholas. For years, a shard of bone from the saint's left little toe encased in a golden locket had sat hidden in the altar to grace the church and bring succor to the faithful. But that hellish fire consumed it all and left behind nothing but smoke and ashes. Some said it was a bad omen and crossed themselves when they saw little Vlad. Old women spat in their bosoms to ward off the evil eye when they passed by the remnants of the church. But Vlad Dracul knew it was all nonsense. The old church was made of wood, and wood burns, doesn't it? Nothing to do with magic.

Anyhow, that was long ago.

When her six weeks of confinement were over, Doamna Cneajna returned to her poor, her churches, and all her other responsibilities as the First Lady of the land.

Vlad Dracul got busy gathering an army to conquer Wallachia's throne. He bought armor and weapons from the Saxons in Kronstadt and Sibiu. He walked every village in the duchies of Amlas and Făgăraș, talking the men into joining his troops. He promised them glory and money, charmed their women, and kissed their babies until he gathered an army of two thousand men and a thousand horses to join him after the harvest. Because no man worth his salt would leave his crop in the fields to go and fight for promises, no matter how sweet the talk.

"Is two thousand enough?" Doamna Cneajna asked.

Vlad shrugged.

"It's all I could get, so it will have to be enough."

When the leaves in the mountains caught fire and the mornings turned frosty in the valleys, the time had come to go. Vlad gathered his men and donned his new shiny armor.

He kissed little Radu, who tried to bite his father's thick, black mustache. Vlad laughed and handed him back to his wet nurse without meeting her eyes.

He hugged little Vlad. "You be a good boy for Mama, will you? Listen to her and do what she tells you."

"Where are you going?"

"I'm going south, to Wallachia, to get our throne."

"Can I come with you?"

"Not this time. You're too young. The men and I are going to war, and war is not a place for children."

"Why not?"

"Because bad things happen at war. People get hurt, and people die."

"I want to see."

Vlad Dracul shook his head. "No, you don't. Even I'd rather not, but I don't have a choice. You stay home and take care of Mama and little Radu, and I'll get you a gift."

"What gift?"

"Something special."

"Can I have the throne?"

Vlad Dracul laughed. "Not just yet. But someday..."

He ruffled his hair and turned to Doamna Cneajna. He kissed both her cheeks and tasted the salt of her tears.

"God willing, I'll send for you soon. Be safe."

"You too," she whispered, hugging him tight and burying her face in his shoulder.

The door slammed behind him as he climbed down the stairs to the cobblestoned street where Mircea waited, holding his horse. Not Dragon, the fire-breathing stallion Sigismund had gifted him. Not even old Viscol, who had retired to spend his days chewing on hay and carrots in the stable. This was one of the surefooted dark ponies with a thick, furry coat his men rode. He was used to crossing the mountains and spending the winter outside.

"This isn't much of a horse," Mircea said. "Not when you have Dragon."

"He's the right horse for the job. Dragon wouldn't make it through the mountains in winter. He's used to a warm stable and plenty of good food. He wouldn't know how to dig for grass and how to eat snow when there's no water. And he'd freeze to death."

Mircea sighed.

"I guess. But he's beautiful."

"He sure is. You know what? When this is all over, I'll let you ride Dragon."

Mircea's face lit like a Christmas tree. "You will?"

"Yes. But I need you to promise me something."

"Anything."

"While I'm gone, you'll be the man of the house. You need to take care of your mother and your brothers. Make sure they're safe from harm. I have nobody else to ask but you."

Mircea shook his head. "You don't need to ask. And you don't need to promise me anything. I know that Mama, Vlad, and Radu are mine to look after, even when you're here. More so when you're not."

"Thank you, my son."

Vlad Dracul hugged him and mounted the horse.

"Father?"

"Yes?"

"You think that woman's curse was real?"

Vlad sighed. "I don't know what I think. But we are all well and healthy, and nothing happened."

"Yet."

"Yet. And hopefully forever."

He nodded to Mircea and tightened his knees to urge the pony forward. A nine-year-old boy shouldn't have to be the man of the house, but they were living in terrible times. They all had to do their best, and Mircea was brave and wise beyond his years.

The old woman's words came to his mind, and a great shiver shook his insides.

"The oldest one, your heir, you'll live to watch him die. He'll die a death, the kind of which you wouldn't wish on your worst enemy. And only after that you'll die, betrayed, broken, and alone."

CHAPTER 23

THE CAMPAIGN

C arpathian Mountains, Zaplaz, 1436

It's been weeks since Vlad Dracul and his men left home, and Vlad misses his family. He also misses the comforts of home: a lively fire, a good dinner, and a soft bed warmed by a loving wife. There's nothing like that here, even though he happened upon a warmed bed or two along the way.

Winter is harsh up here in the Carpathians. It's only October, but everything's frozen and white like it's Christmas as they trudge across the high pass that joins Transylvania to Wallachia. It's hard to say who's got it worse: Vlad's men, or the tiny mountain ponies with their frosted coats, trudging through fresh snow to their knees, bending under the weight of the equipment. The soldiers slip and slide like a bunch of drunks through the slush the horses left behind, with their high double-fur hats pulled over their ears and their frozen hands hidden inside their sheepskin mantles.

Mounted on his surefooted pony, Vlad is everywhere. He trots to the front, waits for the back, and finds a word of encouragement for every man in between. He knows them all by name, and he knows the names of their wives and their children. That's why they all look at him like he's anointed by God.

"Good job you're doing, Ion. Just a couple more hours, and we'll set camp for the night. Tomorrow or the day after, we'll start the descent, and we'll leave this dratted snow behind. No more freezing slush and sleet for us.

"Everything will be easier in the valley, Gheorghe. We'll find dry wood for the fire, a sheep or two to roast, and with a little luck, maybe even some wine down in Rucăr. They must have harvested the grapes by now."

The men don't say much, but their faces light up when they see him next to them and they hear him speak their language.

When the sun finally sinks behind the mountains, and they start making camp, Vlad helps gather wood, sits with them by the fire to listen to their stories, partakes of their bread and cheese, and shares his wine. His eyes moisten with longing for home, just like theirs, when they listen to Ilie, the old shepherd, squeeze love, tears, and sorrow out of his flute.

Only when the fire dies and the men curl to sleep, wrapped in their sheepskin mantles, does Vlad steal a handful of spent ashes to mix with a few drops of wine. He takes a precious piece of paper from his saddlebag and removes the feather from his hat to write home.

> *Our dear Doamna Cneajna.*
> *Thanks to God and all the saints, especially St. Gheorghe, the Dragon Slayer, and our chosen patron, we are well. One more long march through the snow, maybe two, and we'll be past the worst of the Carpathians, which are beautiful but awfully harsh. Last week we lost a horse, who broke his leg stepping into a crevasse, and two*

men. *The young one slid into a ravine. His older brother tried to save him but went down with him instead. We spent hours trying to find them, but we couldn't. So we prayed for the eternal rest of their souls and spilled a drop of wine in their memory, though we don't have much left. As for the horse, the men butchered him, so, for once, we had fresh meat.*

We sent word to the boyars at the court of Târgoviște. We told them that Sultan Murad's doctor lost all hope of helping Alexandru Aldea, who has already received his last rites since he isn't expected to survive the week.

That's not true, of course. The messenger from Edirne that our men caught said that Alexandru is doing better, but the boyars don't need to know that. The more convinced they are that Alexandru is as good as dead, the less likely they will stand with Boyar Albu, that venomous snake who hates our guts. We hope the boyars will see the light and open their arms to us, welcoming us as their rightful voivode, so we can save our arrows and our men to fight our enemies, the faithless Ottomans, instead of spilling the blood of our brothers.

We trust that you and the boys are all well. Every night and every day, we pray to God for your health, strength, and patience and for our boys' health, wisdom, and good luck.

Your God-fearing and always loving husband,

Vlad Dracul

CHAPTER 24
DOAMNA CNEAJNA'S LETTER

Sighişoara, November 1436

My dear husband and prince,

"We are all happy to hear that you are doing well. We are sorry to hear about the loss of your men and the horse, but we are glad you made good use of the meat, and we prayed for the souls of the men.

"Here at home, we started getting ready for Christmas. The women cleaned the house, whitewashed the walls, and scrubbed the floors until the wood shone like golden honey. They beat the carpets outside in the snow and I had the boys walk all over them until no dirt was left.

"The butcher killed the two pigs we'd fattened. We made sausages, hams, and thick slabs of fatty bacon that we brined with salt and herbs, then hung to cold-smoke in the shed. We cooked the rest of the meat in its own fat and arranged it in deep clay jars, then poured the hot grease over it and tied clean linen cloth over it to keep for winter.

The boys are well, always out and about, playing with the silver-

smith's sons and those of the furrier. The other day Vlad whipped the rope-maker's son, so he no longer wants to play with them.

Mircea is a good boy. He looks after the young ones like you told him, but I hope you won't let him ride Dragon like you promised. I know he's a good rider, but he's only nine, and that horse is a devil. Just the other day, he bit the stable boy so bad that he won't go near him anymore, and I had to hire another.

Radu is a joy to have around. He's walking and running now, and he always smiles and laughs, even when he falls. He's such a happy kid unless Vlad is around.

The wet nurse went dry. She somehow managed to get with child, even though it's just us women here — other than the soldiers you left us. She won't tell me who the father was, but judging by the size of her belly, it must have happened before you left. I hope she has a girl.

We all pray every morning and every night for your health, wisdom, and victory. We can't wait to join you in Târgoviște.

Your God-fearing wife,
Doamna Cneajna

CHAPTER 25
THE JOURNEY'S END

November 1436

Months have passed since Vlad Dracul's men put away the harvest, kissed their wives goodbye, and left their homes to join Vlad's army, hoping to build a better life for their children. They've slogged through snow, crossed freezing rivers, and scrambled up and down Carpathian's merciless trails, freezing their assets and sleeping on an empty stomach with only the Good Lord's sky for a cover. Some lost fingers, limbs, and even their lives to frostbite, accidents, and bad luck. But they knew it was worth it.

As soon as they crossed into Wallachia, they'd find food, wine, and women to keep them warm, willingly or not. Because the spoils of war are part of the pay.

Vlad Dracul said no.

"There'll be no looting, no raping, and no roughing up anyone. This is to be my country, and I won't let you burn it to the ground like the Ottomans do. We'll only take what we're given or what we pay for. The Wallachians are our brothers and sisters, and we'll treat them as such."

His men didn't like it.

They frowned and grumbled but pretended to listen. They stole a chicken here and a sheep there, and Vlad Dracul didn't seem to notice. But when a woman came complaining that two of his men had raped her daughter, Vlad Dracul turned purple with fury.

"She was going to marry next summer. But now that she's soiled, no man will want her, even if she's not heavy with child. Her life is over, and our whole family is covered in shame.

"Bring her here. I want to speak to her," Vlad thundered.

The woman shivered but listened. She brought the girl, so wrapped in her headscarf that you couldn't see her face, and pushed her forward toward Vlad. The girl fell to her knees.

The men snickered.

"What's he gonna do to her?" one asked.

"Whip her for lying," someone answered. "Maybe even hang her."

"I don't think so. He's too soft; he'll just give her some money and make her go away."

Vlad acted like he didn't hear them. He helped the girl to her feet and spoke kindly as if she were his daughter.

"I'm sorry this happened to you, but I need you to be brave. Look at my men and tell me: which are the ones that hurt you?"

The girl walked from one man to another. She pointed out two of them.

Vlad turned to the men.

"Is this true?"

The men shrugged. One spat to the side.

"It's not our fault. She was looking for it. Why else would she go alone in the forest at night? We just did what any man would do."

"Not any man," Vlad said.

He gave the girl's mother a small bag of money.

"I know it's not a lot, but it's all I can spare. That should be enough of a dowry to get her married well. I'll pray to God to heal her body and soul. And call me to the wedding. I'll give her away."

He turned to the men.

"You two should have known better, but you didn't listen. The other ones will."

He turned to their captain.

"Hang them both. And leave the bodies hanging so everyone learns what happens when they break my laws."

The men tried to escape, but their comrades took them away.

"You can't do this to us! We served you faithfully all this time," they cried.

But Vlad turned away. In the following days, he pretended not to notice his men's resentment and fear. They no longer saw him as their friend but as their voivode. And that was just fine, as long as they fought for him like they promised.

It didn't take long. A few mornings later, they saw the blue smoke rising from Târgoviște's chimneys, and they knew they'd arrived. The men whispered the Lord's prayer and crossed themselves. They arranged into formation, ready to storm the Târgoviște castle.

"For God. For Country. For Glory," Vlad shouted.

Two thousand voices rose like one.

"For God. For Country. For Glory."

Two thousand hearts drummed in as many chests as Vlad's army wrapped around the castle's timbered walls, hoping this wasn't the last day of their lives. They looked up for arrows flying from the crenels. They listened for the sound of boulders spitting out of the trebuchets. They sniffed for the noxious smell of hot oil pouring over them from above.

Two thousand men wished they'd been kinder to their wives and better fathers to their children. Two thousand soldiers got ready to win or die.

But they didn't.

A white flag rose on top of the watchtower, and the gates opened.

CHAPTER 26

THE THRONE OF THORNS

Târgoviște, November 1436

It's been a rough few months, but the Târgoviște Castle is finally in Vlad Dracul's hands. Boyar Albu, Alexandru Aldea's right-hand man, has made himself scarce. Vlad can only hope that he ran to the Ottomans, so he can declare him a traitor to the country. Then he can condemn him to death and confiscate his lands, fishing ponds, and vineyards to breathe some life into the country's empty coffers.

But most boyars welcomed him with the traditional bread and salt and many false sweet words. They bent the knee and swore fealty. Vlad smiled and thanked them, even though he knew it was a lie. They welcomed him now that he came with his troops, but next time they'll embrace Basarab or whoever else brings an army. But he lied too, and thanked them, because that's how you keep a country together.

They stayed long enough to watch Nifon, Târgoviște's Holy Mitropolit and the highest priest in Wallachia's Orthodox church, smear Vlad's forehead and breast with holy oil to anoint him as Voivode of

Wallachia. Then, the lies all done, they went about their business and left, leaving him free to explore his new castle and savor his win.

Alone in the throne room, Vlad stands in front of the carved wooden chair that his father, Mircea the Elder, ran the country from. The throne is old and cracked and smooth with use and not much different from the high-backed chairs around the dinner table. But it's what he has longed for his whole life. And it's his.

He sits. The wood is hard, and the armrests are too high. The angry eagle carved in the chair's high back pokes him in the ribs instead of hugging him. But it's just like it should be. This is the throne in which his father, and his father's father before him, sat to rule Wallachia from. And it's his.

He'll keep it, God willing, then pass it on to Mircea, then Vlad, and even little Radu, if that witch Smaranda was right. She has yet to be wrong.

He takes it all in — the thick castle walls; the narrow windows letting in thin darts of light; the throne's armrests, smooth under his fingers; the ruckus of church bells ringing all over Târgoviște to celebrate the new voivode; the faint smell of holy basil from the anointment on his chest — and he sighs with relief. He has reached his goal. He's finally home, on the throne where he belongs.

He's still basking in joy when Gheorghe, his right-hand man, steps in.

"A letter from Târgoviște, my voivode."

Vlad looks at the seal. It's not Doamna Cneajna's white wax with the imprint of Moldova's bison from her father's ring. This one's yellow, like the skinny candles you light in church for a copper, and the print... He stares to see what it is, but he can't figure it out.

He shrugs and opens it.

My dear Father and Voivode,

"We are well. I do my best to be a good prince and look after Mother and the boys, like you told me. Mother is doing well, keeping busy as always with the house and the church.

The boys are well too. Radu grows like a weed. He always has a smile on his face. He started walking and even running, and he can already say Mama, Papa, and Cat.

But Vlad...

The other night I heard something and went to Radu's chamber to check on him. I found Vlad choking him, and I had to fight him to unclench his hands from the baby's throat. It turns out that Radu took Vlad's dagger, the Damascus steel one with the ivory handle you gave him, and played with it. Vlad got so mad he tried to kill him.

I'm glad to report that the baby recovered, but I'm worried Vlad will do it again.

That's why I took Radu to sleep in my room. I told Mother that he would wake me up from my nightmares. She gave me a strange look but didn't push it. Still, I thought you should know.

We love you and look forward to joining you soon.

Your faithful, loving son,
Mircea

Vlad drops the letter in his lap and sighs, remembering the old woman's curse. It's been more than a year, but her words are burned in him forever.

"I curse you, Vlad Dracul. From the broken heart of a mother and grandmother that God will listen to, I curse you. I curse you and your sons and their unborn sons from the first to the last. I curse your sons to forever hate each other."

He shivers. His hand jumps to the hilt of his sword, but there's no one to fight. There's nobody here but him, sitting on the throne of Wallachia like he should. And there's no such thing as a curse. That was nothing but a crazy woman's empty words. They mean nothing. He'll send for Doamna Cneajna and the boys, and they'll be fine. Radu will grow and take care of himself, and little Vlad will outgrow his little fits of anger and learn to behave like a man. So there.

Vlad Dracul claps his hands to ask for paper for his letter when he feels someone watching him. He looks around.

There's nothing.

But still...

He looks up.

Way up above, hanging upside down from the iron chandelier, a bat is watching him.

CHAPTER 27

THE FAMILY'S ARRIVAL

Târgovişte, Spring 1437

The Royal Court of Târgovişte buzzes like a swarming hive. Chatty women with black headscarves and sharp eyes that don't miss a thing open every window, sweep every room, and polish the massive dining table until it glows like gold. Crafty spiders who spent their lives building their corner webs strong enough to trap the voivode of all flies squeeze into the cracks, swearing revenge to the evil brooms that destroyed their livelihood. Stable boys poke fun at each other as they clean the horse stalls from the petrified leftovers of long-dead horses. Clucky chickens run for their lives to escape the hungry hands chasing them to put them in the pot.

Vlad Dracul paces back and forth in the long courtyard, where most of the snow has already melted in the sun, and listens to the ruckus. Oh, how he wishes that the messenger from Buda hadn't arrived today, of all days. Today was supposed to be for joy and celebration. God knows he worked hard to earn it. He didn't need that darned scroll he squeezed inside his belt to ruin the family reunion.

Because today Doamna Cneajna and the children are supposed to arrive. They left Sighişoara as soon as he sent for them, but it took them weeks to get here. No wonder. The heavy oxen carts loaded with everything they owned had a hard time cutting through the Carpathians. Then little Radu got sick, and they had to stay put until he got better. Then the snow closed the roads. But now they're finally here, thank God. Vlad Dracul's heart is full of love and longing, and he pushes the bad news aside. There'll be plenty of time for that later.

"They're here!" shouts the watcher in the tower, and the fuss stops. No matter their job, the folks at the court drop it like it's hot and align in front of the gates to greet their new Lady and the princes.

Vlad's heart urges him to go and meet them, but he holds back. This is their moment of glory, and God knows they've earned it, keeping everything together throughout the time he's been gone. So he hides in the shade of a column to wait, though he doesn't need to. Nobody pays him any mind. They're all excited like children told it's Christmas.

A woman pretends to spit in her bosom to ward off the evil eye.

"Ptiu! Look at him! Isn't he the spitting image of his father? And look at that white stallion! That's a fire-breathing dragon if I ever saw one."

"That's got to be Mircea, the eldest. He's a good-looking kid, for sure! But won't you just look at that baby? Blond, blue-eyed, and smiling, he looks like baby Jesus in the icons."

"That's the youngest one, Radu. Look at him laugh and wave at us like he knows us."

"What a happy kid. Not like the other, riding the gray horse. Good rider, for sure, but look at that frown! It's like he got weaned on piss and vinegar. What's his problem, I wonder?"

"I bet he doesn't like playing second fiddle to his brothers. If looks could kill, that baby would be with the angels."

"There's the carriage. That's got to be Doamna Cneajna. They say she's as beautiful as a spring day."

"She's got to be. How else would you get that pretty blond baby out of the Draculas?"

The sound of the horses' hooves grows louder. Seconds later, Mircea prances in the courtyard riding Dragon with little Radu in his lap.

His eyes moist with tears, Vlad Dracul opens his arms.

"Father!"

Mircea jumps off. Vlad closes his arms around his two sons, his heart so full of love it could burst.

"Mircea. Radu. I'm so glad you're here."

He kisses Mircea's cheeks, lifts little Radu on his shoulders, and turns to greet Vlad. But Vlad has no use for his greeting. His face scrunched in anger, he stares at little Radu like he's a venomous snake, not a cute chubby baby.

"I see you greeted him first," Vlad says, jumping off Viscol and heading inside without touching his father.

Vlad sighs but lets him be. He heads to help Doamna Cneajna out of her carriage. She looks pale and tired, but her green velvet dress is embroidered with pearls, and her neck and hands are heavy with gold, as it befits the new Lady of Wallachia. She submits to Vlad's hug without warmth, and his heart skips a beat. Has she learned the news already? Or is there more bad news he doesn't know?

"Welcome home, my lady," Vlad says.

Doamna Cneajna's smile doesn't quite reach her eyes, but she waves and thanks the onlookers before heading inside.

CHAPTER 28

NEWS FROM AFAR

V lad Dracul sighs. May as well be done with this.

"What happened, my lady? What angered you so? Who spread lies that poisoned your soul?"

Doamna Cneajna's mouth tightens into a line.

"You dare speak about lies?"

"But..."

The ruckus next door interrupts him. There's shouting and crying and metal clanging on metal like in a sword fight. Vlad rushes over with Doamna Cneajna on his heels.

"What in God's name...."

Standing in the middle of the throne room, Vlad holds his wrist. He glares at Mircea, who's about to slip his sword into its scabbard. His cheeks wet with tears, little Radu clings to the throne.

"What happened?" Doamna Cneajna asks.

Mircea shrugs. "Vlad, as usual. Radu tried to crawl up on the throne, and Vlad took his sword out to cut him."

Vlad Dracul blanches.

"Is that true, Vlad?"

Vlad's brow furrows in anger.

"It's not my fault. He shouldn't have tried to take the throne. You said you'd go first, then Mircea, then me. It wasn't his turn."

Vlad Dracul shakes his head.

"Are you kidding me? Were you going to kill the baby for trying to crawl onto a chair? He doesn't know it's the throne. He doesn't even know what a throne is. He's just a baby, for God's sake. He's barely two!"

Vlad shrugs.

"Then stop him from taking my stuff. He always takes what's mine: my bow, my dagger, and now my throne. Make it stop."

"You try to hurt him even when he's not doing anything to you, just because," Mircea said. "You hate him."

"Sure I do. Don't you?" Vlad shrieks.

"I..."

"That's enough!" Vlad Dracul thunders. "Vlad, go to your room and stay there until I come for you. Mircea, take Radu and look after him while I speak to your mother."

The boys go. The throne room gets eerily quiet, and the silence is God-awful heavy.

Doamna Cneajna sighs.

"That's how it's been since you left. Every day. I'm afraid we've had one boy too many. And speaking about boys…"

"What?"

"Radu's wet nurse, the buxom one? The one who fell dry? She had a boy. Dark-haired and green-eyed. He's your spitting image. She named him Vlad."

Vlad Dracul sighs. That was one thing he didn't need today. But it is what it is.

"I'm sorry."

"I bet. One more contender to my sons' throne. Like there aren't plenty already. And why? Just because you can't keep your boots under your own bed."

"I'm sorry, Doamna Cneajna. I really am. But I promise I'll make sure he's no threat to our sons. I swear."

"How? What are you going to do? Kill him?"

Vlad Dracul shakes his head.

"No. But when he's old enough, I'll send him to a monastery to be a monk and a man of God. He'll be no threat to our boys, you'll see. Now to my news. I'm afraid it's worse."

"Worse? Worse than our sons trying to kill each other and your whore popping out another bastard?"

"I'm afraid so."

Doamna Cneajna pales.

"What is it?"

"I just got a messenger from Buda. King Sigismund, our lord and protector who helped us take Wallachia, is dead. Our powerful ally is no more."

Doamna Cneajna's brow furrows.

"I'm sad to hear that. But he was an old man. And you've got your throne already. So..."

Vlad Dracul shakes his head.

"You don't understand. Sigismund's dead. Albert, his successor, is too busy trying to secure his own throne to help me, even if he wanted to. And Basarab, that venomous snake, is already eyeing the Wallachian throne. War is coming."

THE END

Dear Reader, thank you for reading my book. If you loved it, please take a moment and **leave a review** to help others discover it. That means a lot to me.

Sign up for my newsletter at **RRJonesBooks.com** for more updates and freebies, including some finger-licking Transylvanian recipes.

And if you're curious about what came next for Vlad, Radu and Mircea, read RRJones's ***Den of Spies***.

ABOUT THIS BOOK

This book was an afterthought.

I'd already written three lengthy tomes about the Dracula brothers and their complicated relationship when I thought about writing this prequel. It was meant as a little teaser to entice readers. A few pages, a couple of days' work.

I started researching Vlad Dracul's life. Then I fell in love.

This book happened not because of me but despite me. The more I learned about Vlad Dracul's cunning, determination, and ruthless struggle for Wallachia's throne, the more I wanted to know.

So I made time and ended up with more than the short story I'd planned. I discovered a cast of fascinating characters that shaped the Draculas' lives and peeked into Transylvania's mysterious magic. More of that to come.

I hope you enjoyed it.

ABOUT THE AUTHOR

RR Jones was born in Transylvania, near Bran Castle, where deep forests keep dark secrets, Dracula's spirit inhabits the six-foot thick walls, and long strings of garlic adorn the houses' windows.

She learned about magic from her grandma. She skipped school to chase ghosts around the old towers' ruins and roamed the Carpathians, breathing in their pine incense and their magic.

But that was long ago. These days, she lives in the Adirondacks. She spends her days reading, kayaking, and hiking with her German shepherd Guinness. But she still has a black cat named Paxil. And a broom that doesn't get much use. She'd rather walk.

Transylvania's history and magic run deep in her blood, so she pours them into her books.

Find more at RRJonesBooks.com.

DEN OF SPIES

EXCERPT

Kronstadt, Transylvania, 1442

Ana approaches one of the guards. They're so big their halberds alone are twice her size. She's about to ask about the kitchens when he looks down at her and shakes his head.

"You're late. What took you so long? They've already gathered in the Red Tower. You're the last one. Come on, I'll take you there."

He heads to the drawbridge leading to the tower, and Ana has to run to keep up. He crosses it in two steps, then pushes the iron-studded door and heads down a dark stone hallway. Ana's right behind him as he opens the door to a vast room.

"There."

He pushes her forward and slams the door shut.

Ana tries to say something, but it's too late. He's gone.

Oh well.

She turns to see a hundred kids staring at her.

The stone room is gray and cold and so enormous that the village church and the cemetery could fit in, with room left over. But it's alive with the flickering flames of the sizzling torches. And empty, but for the kids.

They're all peasants, dressed like her in thick white pants held up with wide belts, long-sleeved embroidered white tunics, and open sheepskin vests. Their tall fur hats fall over their ears, just like hers. So why do they stare at her like she's weird?

She scratches her head and notices her hat's missing. She must have lost it while she chased the guard. Now, her thick chestnut braid falls over her shoulder, betraying she's a girl.

She takes a deep breath and straightens, standing up as tall as a scrawny, five feet tall girl can get, and pulls her stomach in, hoping the boys won't hear it growl. And if they do, so what?

She clenches her jaw to stop her teeth from chattering and takes it all in. Most boys are bigger than her, but the room dwarfs them all. Way above, its ceiling fade in the darkness. The three feet thick cold walls are rarely broken by narrow dark windows like blind eyes.

And it's evil.

Ana knows these stones have crushed women's hopes, drank men's blood, and destroyed children's futures. These cruel walls are imbued with sorrows and secrets. Ana feels it in her bones and shivers.

She wishes she was closer to the fire roaring at the short end of the room in a fireplace large enough to roast a whole boar. But there's no boar, just a blistering tree trunk spitting sparks, so hot that the grill glows red, burring the air.

The two Saxons sitting by the fire are the only grown-ups in the room. They murmur to each other, watching the kids.

Why not?

Ana drifts towards the fire. A few more steps, and she's close enough to warm her hands and hear the men chat.

"What do you think?" The tall one rests his chin on his hand. His restless fingers tap his jaw, setting the ruby in his ring on fire.

The fat one shrugs and wipes the sweat off his forehead with his gold-embroidered sleeve. His hooded eyes slip from one kid to the other.

He's too close to the fire. And he hasn't missed many meals, Ana thinks, then hushes her mind back to her task. She's not here to judge anyone, not even fat Saxons. She's here to eat.

"I don't know what to say, burgomaster. It's way too early," he answers. Then his eyes fall on Ana, and he startles.

"That one! That one's a girl. What on earth are you going to do with her?"

The burgomaster's sharp eyes turn to her. His thick brows come together, and he opens his mouth to say something, but he doesn't. A smile spreads on his face, and he chuckles.

"You're right, Karl. That's a girl. Isn't that something? So what? Girl – boy – what does it matter? As long as they're bright, strong, and loyal?"

Karl stutters.

"But look at her! She's smaller than a field mouse and only half that pretty, with that silly mop of chestnut hair. What do you think you'll do with her?"

"Don't forget that women can sometimes go where the best men can't. Even more so at the sultan's court. How many uncut men ever got inside the Edirne Sarayi and lived to tell the tale?

Karl shakes his head.

"Come on, burgomaster. Say you got her there somehow – I don't see how, but let's say you did. Then what? No woman leaves the harem alive. Not even the validé, the sultan's mother, Once she's there, she'll be there till the day she dies. You're just wasting your time and our money."

"Only if they know she's a girl."

The fat man grins.

"If she's not a girl and not a boy, what will she be? A peacock?"

"Close. How about a eunuch?"

Karl chokes.

"A eunuch? She doesn't look like a eunuch. She can't be a eunuch."

"I'll bet you a thousand ducats."

"You're out of your mind. I'll bet you a hundred."

"Deal."

What's a eunuch? Ana wonders.

To learn what happened to Ana, Vlad, and Radu, get your copy of DEN OF SPIES today.